THE DEATH OF RUTH

ELIZABETH KATA, born in Australia, lived for many years in Japan. Married in Tokyo in 1937 her son was born in a mountain village just three weeks before the atomic bomb was dropped on Hiroshima.

Her first novel, *A Patch of Blue,* has been translated into eight different languages and was made into an award-winning film. Her second novel, set in war-time Japan, has been purchased by an American film company.

Elizabeth Kata also writes screenplays for film and television. Her work has been produced in Australia, the United Kingdom and the United States.

She is presently living in Sydney.

THE
DEATH
OF
RUTH

by

Elizabeth Kata

For Sue
from
Elizabeth Kata

Pan Books Sydney and London

Sydney.

First published 1981 by Pan Books (Australia) Pty Limited
1 Castlereagh Street, Sydney
© Elizabeth Kata 1981

National Library of Australia
Cataloguing-in-Publication data
Kata, Elizabeth
  The death of Ruth
  ISBN 0 330 27017 6
  I. Title
A823'.3

Printed and bound in Australia by The Dominion Press, Melbourne

CHAPTER ONE

IT SEEMS AEONS since I had awakened with the usual
bewilderment of mind which accompanies one's return
to consciousness. I had smiled, happy and complacent,
knowing that John would be returning from his business
trip in several days time. I had smiled, looking forward to
the hours we would spend talking about his work and
about the everyday happenings of my life whilst he had
been away; knowing that when he returned, I would
follow my time-honoured habit, hiding the fact that I was
always fearful and nervous during his absence, especially
since the recent robbery; and then, as always, when night
came and we were together in our bed, in the dark, I would
restrain myself and follow along with John in our temp-
erate and gentle love-making.

I have never let him know the extent of the love I feel
towards him. John, I have always felt, could be repelled by
too strong a show of passion. It had always been my pride,
my endeavour, to be his perfect wife and helpmate in every
way.

It scarcely seems possible now, that I had lain in my bed,
allowing my mind to dwell on homely, pleasant things, that
I had been seriously thinking about having a dark rinse on
my greying hair and hoping, that if I did, John would
approve. That is what I had been thinking when the sudden
outburst of raised voices had interrupted my thoughts,
causing me to burrow beneath the coverlet and cover my
ears . . .

Those raised voices! Those sounds of violence! For
eleven years, ever since the Moyston family moved next

door to become our neighbours, I have suffered those disturbing sounds. For eleven long years I have suffered guilt knowing that Ruth Moyston was a sadistic and a cruel woman — a child basher.

Always, I had felt ashamed of my lack of courage, ashamed of my unwillingness to go against John's advice because I knew that he was correct in saying that if I openly accused Ruth of cruelty to her children, she not only could, but most definitely would sue me for defamation of character.

Once, in a state of desperation, I had spoken to a doctor about 'someone I had heard of' who beat her children and injured them. I had sought his advice on the matter, and he, the doctor, had advised me to let well alone, that is — he had said — unless the mother could be coerced into putting herself under a psychiatrist's care, 'The mother is the one in need of treatment. *She* is the one in need of help . . .' he had insisted.

Clearly, he, the doctor, like John, had no desire to be involved.

I had tried to encourage Ruth to seek aid, God knows, but never frankly, never openly and bravely, because I was nervous and afraid of her reactions to my interference. But, I had tried even if to no avail, and the beatings, the punishments had continued. The injuries to the children had been skilfully concealed or explained away with, 'Jodie is accident prone . . .'

'Rob is all boy! What boy doesn't collect bruises, break a bone or two . . .?'

Ruth took care not to go too far in her treatment towards the children when Ralph, her husband, was present, and John seemed never to be at home when any serious assault took place.

Right from the beginning, Ruth had regarded me as a weakling. In a way, I had become one of her victims, and she had been aware of that, knowing that I suffered greatly, not as the children suffered but nevertheless painfully and with feelings of guilt.

If I had known of any official organization to approach, I would have written to them anonymously and I would have reported her. I knew about the Society for the Prevention of Cruelty to Animals but of no such society for the prevention of cruelty to children.

The ugly business that went on in the Moyston household had been the only blot on the happiness of my life. I had heard, watched and put up with the ugliness for years, so why — why and oh why — now that Rob and Jodie were in their early teens, and able to stand up for themselves, why did I lose control of myself that morning?

Whilst lying in my bed I had been completely overcome with anger and disgust on hearing Ruth's strident voice screaming out obscenities, and on hearing Jodie's voice raised in panic and pain, screaming, 'No, no, please Mother, no more! *No more . . .!*'

I lay trembling, filled with ever rising fury until eventually I heard Jodie running from the house and along the road on her way to school. Acting on impulse, I sprang from my bed, dragged a house-coat over my nightdress and hurried over to the Moystons' house.

As usual, Ruth's transistor radio was blaring forth on full volume and she, Ruth, was standing at her kitchen sink drinking down a dose of the medicine she used to quieten her nerves, to relieve her acid stomach condition.

'Ruth,' I exclaimed loudly, 'I have come to warn you.'

Ruth, with her usual insolence, ignored me and kept her back toward me. Angered by her attitude, I stepped further into the room, raising my voice, crying out, 'I won't stand for it any longer! You are cruel, *vicious*, and . . .'

As though she was standing on a swivelling platform, Ruth swung about to face me. Alarmed — very alarmed — because she was obviously about to attack me, I stepped back a pace or two, as she, with her arms raised, lunged towards me. With all the force I was able to muster I fended her off — pushing her. She slipped, falling backwards on to the tiled floor to lie there, prostrate and silent.

With all anger evaporated, I crouched down beside her, distraught, calling her name again and yet again and I noticed that blood was seeping from a wound in the back of her head.

The sight of that blood unnerved me, made me dizzy. The room seemed to darken, then to become frighteningly light and bright. Steadying my mind I gazed down at Ruth's distorted face and — with horror — I believed that she was dead.

As though frozen, I remained in my crouching position and my mind became kaleidoscopic, a shambles of terrifying visions. Visions of myself, Molly Blake — not only being held responsible for having caused my neighbour's death, but being accused of having killed her with intent.

No, no, no, I reasoned, that could not happen. Not to me! But — maybe it could! Yes, it could, but it would be macabre, too incredible and I would not stand for it! I had every right to protect myself — protect my reputation, my wonderfully happy, orderly life with John.

There was no way that anyone could prove that I had been with Ruth when she died. Ralph had left the house for work. Rob had left the house for school. Jodie had run weeping from the house quite some minutes before my arrival. Surely I had every right to protect myself! Yes. I would go home. Behave as usual. Make an appointment with the hairdresser . . .

No one could suspect a woman who sat, calmly, having her hair shampooed, tinted and set, of having killed a person earlier on in the day. Killed? Dear God it was not fair, Ruth, not I, had always been the violent one. Ruth had attacked *me*.

But — she was dead! I was responsible for her death and I knew I would have to face up to that terrible fact, and face up to the notoriety, the scandal. I convinced myself I would face up to it. I would, but I needed time! I would go home, calm down, clear my mind, then call and notify the police from my own home.

It was at that moment, with a shock that I saw Ruth's blood was staining the hem of my floral house-coat and as I leapt to my feet a further shock shattered me completely as the Moystons' telephone bell began to shrill out.

I ran — as though being pursued — from Ruth's kitchen and out into the sunlit brightness of the morning. I ran on through the Moystons' neglected back yard, and with an ease which even in my panic impressed me, I climbed over the low fence that separated our properties, then, I ran on through the cultivated neatness of John's back yard and into the sanctuary of my own home.

Home! Safe! Surrounded by familiar objects, I was enveloped by a remarkable calm.

I felt that there was no tragedy in Ruth being dead but that if I were associated in any way with the cause of her death then it would be tragic, it would cause chaos, and a multitude of painful embarrassments. It could cause John's and my way of life to crumble — be destroyed! I needed, I longed for John, and I had cried out, 'Oh John if only you were not away.'

Just thinking of my husband brought on a desperate burst of weeping. Always, when John has been away on business trips I have felt like a boat cut adrift from its moorings. Even small problems took on exaggerated proportions and the smooth flow of my life became disrupted.

I knew I should call the police and inform them that a death had occurred, and I knew I would do that. But still, I needed more time, just a little more time.

Taking off my blood stained house-coat I soaked it in cold water, and clad in my nightgown, I went into the bedroom.

I crept into our bed. I lay upon the new mattress which John and I had so recently and proudly purchased and pulling the covers over my head I curled up and, in the warmth and the darkness — as though watching the replay of a film — the events of the morning flashed and flickered before my eyes.

I began to reason that in a macabre way I had done Ruth Moyston a favour. True, she was dead but she had hated her life.

Then, as though I were on a see-saw, I changed my mind, knowing that I must behave with decency and honesty. But — what would John, what would our small circle of friends, think of me? Why should I stain my good reputation? How dreadful if I were to be dragged through an inquest, a . . .? The mere thought of such things was unendurable to me. I would not call the police. I would go about my day as though nothing unusual had happened.

Unusual? But — Ruth was *dead*.

Then I heard the sound of a motor vehicle driving along the street. I knew that it would be the baker's van. He, the baker, came every second day. So, let *him* discover Ruth's body. Let *him* give the alarm. He always went to the Moystons' first and when he came to my house I would be ready for him. I would be . . .

Leaping from the bed I felt beneath my pillow for my handkerchief. It was not there. I knew where it would be! I had carried it, crushed in my hand, when I had gone over to speak to Ruth. Had I dropped it on her kitchen floor? That initialled handkerchief could be my undoing.

Once again I was impressed with the speed, with the dexterity I garnered as I ran, climbed, ran again.

When the delivery boy finally arrived, I was home again, in my living room, on my knees, shaking and trembling with my handkerchief retrieved, and with the key of the Moystons' back door cutting into my hand, and when the boy called to me from my back door I answered him, my

10

voice high, calm and rational, calling, 'Just leave me one sliced loaf, Ted. Mr Blake is still away you know!'

'Rightio!' he yelled, 'Hey, Mrs Blake, did Mrs Moyston tell you how many loaves she wants today?'

'No,' I called, 'she didn't.' I added, 'Isn't she at home?'

'Well, I'm not sure,' he said, 'The back door is locked but all the front windows are wide open and her radio is going full blast.'

'Maybe she is taking a shower,' I called, 'You may leave her usual order in my kitchen, Ted.'

'OK,' he yelled cheerily, and I listened as he whistled his way down the side path. I heard his van drive off, then I began to weep. I wept shamefully, hopelessly, longing for John, and the thought of John caused me to weep even more. I could not endure the thought that he would have to know of my irrational actions. I could not bear that thought, and as I wept, another thought crept into my mind. I thought how wonderful it would be if only that body was not lying on that floor.

If only that body was not lying on that floor . . . If only . . .

The thought obsessed me — took over completely. I wanted to cause that body to disappear magically — to hide it away.

I was weeping again, and as I wept I sweated and dug with maniacal strength in John's garden. I dug and fought my way into the yielding earth as I had never imagined a person could dig and fight and when the trench was deep enough I knew that I must continue on because it was not yet long enough.

As I dug and wept a medley of thoughts and visions flitted and flooded in and out of my demented mind.

. . .A good thing — now — that our two houses were so isolated. Good thing the real estate man had bought and pulled down all the other houses in the vicinity . . .

. . .A good thing — now — that I had kept my old shorts and tennis shoes instead of giving them away in a charity bundle. Wise of me to have worn my old brown cotton gloves when I had gone back to the Moystons' house. Oh — cruel and sad to have uprooted John's three recently purchased and much treasured camellia bushes . . .

. . .How strange I felt! So light-headed and yet so strong! More like a robot than a human being . . . Strange how I had scarcely bothered to glance at Ruth's body as I had run past it and on into her bedroom . . .

. . .Again I saw myself pulling and dragging the shabby old travelling case from the top of Ruth's wardrobe. It had been filled with musty books confiscated from her children. I had tipped them, helter-skelter, on to the almost thread-bare carpet . . .

. . .I had packed as many of Ruth's belongings as was possible into the case. Had I forgotten anything? I had packed her two good dresses, most of her underwear. Her bathrobe needed laundering and it was bulky but she would never have gone off and left it behind. In it had gone, along with her blue velvet jewel case . . .

. . .Had I made certain that her string of cultured pearls, her cameo brooch and ugly onyx ring were in the case? Yes. And the framed photograph of Rob and Jodie and the box of unused handkerchiefs with its birthday greeting card attached, which read, 'To Mother from Rob and Jodie'.

Gloves, shoes, raincoat . . .

. . .But — her handbag! I had searched and searched. I would have to find it. Have to search for it once more . . .

As I wept and dug I thought of Ralph Moyston. Ralph, always so patient, so gentle. I thought of Rob and Jodie. Their lives always so miserable, so unhappy.

As I wept and dug I thought how wonderful it would have been if Ruth had actually kept her word and had really left home, as for years she had been threatening to. 'I'm clearing out! Leaving you all! Leaving this lousy life! Going off to make a life for myself!' Yes, that had been her oft-repeated threat and if she had actually gone no one would have been greatly amazed, and surely Ralph, for all his goodness, could have only feelings of relief. 'Ruth has left home!' he would say.

'Mother has run away, left home!' Rob and Jodie would say.

'John,' I would say, 'Ruth Moyston has actually cleared out — left home!' And John would shrug and say, 'My goodness! She has? Good *riddance*!'

Yes, if Ruth had, in fact, gone away that is exactly what would have happened.

Twice, during my digging, telephone bells had rung out. The first call had been from my sister, Madge, my invalid sister. Always so fond of long gossips. I had taken a long, steadying breath before explaining, untruthfully, to her that I was in the midst of shampooing my hair.

Some minutes after that call, clambering from the hole I suspended work and waited — spade in hand — listening to the demanding telephone signal shrilling out from the Moystons' house. On and on it went, then, it had ceased. Jumping down into the hole again, I wrenched my ankle. The pain was excruciating, agonizing, but I carried on because time was passing and there were so many urgent and terrible things to be done.

Finally, sweat-soaked, exhausted, and with rank-smelling soil covering me from head to toe, I went hobbling and moaning with pain, to my bathroom. I stripped myself naked and standing beneath the shower I watched the earth-stained water run into the drain.

Without bothering to towel myself, I went into my bedroom and opening a drawer I took up from the lavender-scented sachet, John's last birthday gift to me, a pair of snow-white doe skin gloves. I put them on in place of the now ruined brown cotton gloves I had been wearing, then I snatched up my soiled shorts and shirt and dragged them on.

Ignoring the pain in my ankle, still refusing to recognize

the loathsome nature of my actions and intentions, I crossed over to the Moyston house again. As I swiftly limped my way I realized that I must have stayed beneath the shower for quite a long time. The position of the sun warned me that it was later than I had thought.

Where was the key to the back door? In the pocket of my shorts? Yes. Opening the door I crept into the Moystons' kitchen as a female voice, loud and strident, was proclaiming that she was *more* than pleased with her purchases at a discount furniture shop. Then, crashingly loud, music took over.

The kitchen was empty. Ruth's body no longer lay on the floor.

I stood swaying in the black mist that flooded the room. I wanted to stay in the blackness and the mist, but dragging myself to the sink I picked up a drinking glass that stood on the chipped draining board. It had the remnants of Ruth's stomach mixture in it, she always used it to calm her nerves. Maybe it could help calm me, I needed calming more than ever before in my life.

As I raised the glass to my lips it slipped from my shaking hand and fell on to the tiled floor and the splintering, shattering sound cleared my mind. Common sense told me that Ruth had not died, that the heavy fall had injured, stunned her, and on regaining consciousness she had been able to get up, walk, crawl . . .

Then — where was she? Somewhere in the house? Hiding, frightened of me? Had she watched, as I had dug that grave?

Had *Ruth* called the police? Was she waiting for them to arrive, to charge me for my attack on her and my peculiar activity in John's garden? For having packed that suitcase?

My heart began to chatter with a new fear. The fear of Ruth Moyston — alive. She would see to it that I suffered for my outrageous actions and she had every right on her side and I would be asked *why* I had dug that hole .

During all the years of my marriage I had not so much as planted a seed. I knew that I must fill that gaping hole in — now — at once, before anyone came.

I felt a great tenderness towards myself, digging that now unnecessary hole must have damaged my heart; it ached, my entire body ached. It was not fair that I should have become so embroiled in my neighbour's problems, not fair at all, and it wasn't fair that from some inner source I must find fresh courage, strength enough to cross the garden, climb the fence, fill the hole in and . . .

But first, I must find Ruth. Suddenly and for the first time ever, I admitted to myself that I had hated Ruth for years. She had intimidated Jodie and Rob, she had crippled and crushed the spirit of her husband and from now on she would have the power to intimidate me. The realization frightened me, but that was not important. Just thank God, she, Ruth, was not dead, she was alive. All I had to do was find and face up to her, bravely.

Ruth was lying stretched out on her bed. Her head was turbaned in a gaily coloured bath towel. Her hands were folded together and resting on her bosom and her eyes were closed. She looked quite splendid in a strange kind of way and I was certain that she would be out to scare me, to pretend that she was in a bad way and insist that I call a doctor to see her.

'Ruth . . .?' I whispered from the doorway, 'Ruth it's me — Molly!'

She did not answer. She did not move. As I crossed over to the bed I felt that she was play-acting and determining not to let her upset me too much, I spoke, firmly, saying 'Look at me, Ruth! Come on now . . .' and I took her hand in mine.

I knew, at once, that she was dead.

She must have regained consciousness, struggled through the house, managed to get to her bed only to die there. Once more fear and terror assailed my mind. I knew that come what may, I had to call for help and that meant calling the police. Yes. Yes, and I would call them! Right now and at once.

As I turned away from the bed a new terror struck into my heart. Someone had entered the house. Someone had switched the radio off and in the silence I heard footsteps coming towards the bedroom and then a man's voice called, 'Ruth? Ruth?'

It was Ralph Moyston!

'Ruth? Ruthie, it's me, dear . . .' he was calling apologetically.

Clenching my hands into fists I pressed them against my mouth and I remained that way, listening, as Ralph made his way from room to room, calling Ruth's name, his voice tentative, nervous.

Fraught with fear, with uncertainty, I wondered if I could tell him I had just come over and discovered his wife lying on the bed, lifeless. Could I tell him that? Would he believe me?

Ralph's slight figure appeared in the bedroom doorway. Startled, his gaze went from me to the figure on the bed, than back again to me.

'Molly?' he queried, 'What has happened? What is going on?'

I stared at Ralph with a passionate interest, he stared back, bewildered, and we stared at one another for a long time — a very long time — then again, like a mechanized puppet, he repeated my name.

Still, I was incapable of speaking, of moving. The silence grew unbearable and as Ralph stepped forward I held up a hand, as though to ward him off and I whispered, 'Ralph — Ruth is dead.'

With a rapid movement he covered his face with both hands and just as rapidly I sprang towards him pulling his hands away. His face resembled that of a child, uncomprehending, yet certain of trouble to come as he pushed me aside and moved towards the bed whispering, 'No, no, oh God, *no* . . .'

He peered down into Ruth's face, as he held one of her lifeless hands. Then he turned to face me and I saw that tears were squeezing from his eyes and that blood trickled from his lower lip where his teeth had broken the flesh. He reached out and caught my arm in a painful grip. Terrified, I thought, that now *he*, Ralph, was out to injure me, and struggling to free myself I cried out, 'I didn't mean to hurt her. I didn't mean to kill her . . .

He listened — still grasping my arm — with his head moving from side to side as though trying to clear his mind as I gabbled on incoherently, telling how it had been, how I had heard Ruth beating Jodie, how Ruth had been about to attack me, how I had pushed Ruth, how I had meant to call the police, how I had been too cowardly, too terrified.

'The police?' Ralph's voice broke into my crazed monologue, 'Why the police? You should have called the *doctor*.'

'No!' I interrupted, 'I believed that she was dead. I was sure that she was dead.'

I began to weep bitterly and I wished that Ralph were not so timid and gentle. I wished that he were a man to take command. A man like . . .

But I did not want to think of John . . .

I realized that Ralph had let go of my arm and that he was again peering down at Ruth. 'Molly,' he ground out the words, 'Molly, you have done what I have so often been tempted to do. I might have done it on purpose, you did it accidentally.'

He began moving about the room, waving his hands, crying out, 'You stood up to her! My boy and girl have always despised my lack of courage. *You* stood up to her.'

I was beginning to have the eerie feeling that Ruth could

17

hear, that she was watching us, about to rise up, accusingly, and I cried out, 'Stop wasting time. Call the police. Help me. I can't do it! I am played out.'

I watched Ralph steadying his befuddled mind. Watched as he lifted the receiver of the extension telephone on the bedside table and a new level of fear rose up in me for he — all at once — became aware that except for the telephone, the usually cluttered table top was bare. His eyes flew about the room, taking in the pile of books on the floor, the open and overflowing suitcase. As his eyes questioned mine, in astonishment, a flood of shame enveloped me, as without unlocking my gaze from his, I said, tremulously, 'I — Ralph, I packed her belongings! Packed all Ruth's things . . .' I gestured towards the suitcase.

'But . . .' Ralph stammered, 'But — why?'

'I lost my reason. I was beside myself with fear, afraid that the police, that John, that you, *everyone*, would think I had meant to kill her. I know I must have been out of my mind because I was going to make it appear as though Ruth had left home. Yes, I have been out of my mind with fear.'

Still holding the telephone receiver, Ralph stood gazing into space as though time was of no consequence. Then, abruptly replacing the receiver back on to its cradle, he folded his arms and stared into space again.

'Ralph?' I barely breathed his name, but he heard and looked at me, as I said, 'The *police*?' Again I barely breathed the words, 'Ralph, aren't you going to . . .?' I pointed, childishly, towards the telephone.

'No.' said Ralph, his voice was toneless. 'No. She is dead. Nothing can change that.' Then, all at once, he became distraught, whispering, 'Molly, you must help me.'

'What? I? Help *you* . . .?'

'Yes, help lift! Carry . . .' He gestured to the body on the bed, saying, '*You* said that the head is injured? We don't want blood about the place. We will take her to your place, leave her there until we have time to . . .'

I drew back, horrified, whispering, 'No, no — not to *my* house.'

Ralph ignored my protest, saying, 'Yes, your house! John is still away. Tonight you will be alone there. Molly, it will give us time to think, to plan . . .'

He ran from the room, then he returned carrying a towel, handing it to me saying, 'I can't! You do it, Molly! Make quite sure that . . .'

He turned his back on the bed. He could not bear the sight of blood. I knew that, but neither could I, nevertheless I gathered together the remnants of my strength and when I had completed that which I had to do, Ruth's entire head was covered from view, her face no longer seen.

As we carried our grotesque bundle through the house, moving towards the back door, sweat ran down Ralph's face and the material of my blouse clung damply to my back.

'Faster, move faster,' pleaded Ralph and in trying to obey, I came down heavily on my injured ankle, and a vicious spasm of pain caused me to scream, to let go my part of the burden and point to my ankle. It had swollen to a frightening degree. 'I can't walk on it.' I cried. 'You'll have to manage alone.'

'All right,' he panted, 'All right, all right.' He continued on alone dragging the heavy body across the kitchen floor with his words coming in bursts, saying, 'Molly, *you* bring the case! Bring anything else you see! Her wristwatch! It will be on the shelf over the kitchen sink! Her handbag? *Find her handbag!* She would never go off without that . . .'

'I can't find it,' I sobbed, 'I searched, I searched and searched.'

'You *must* find it.'

'I have already looked everywhere.' I ceased speaking because Ralph was already out of the house.

Painfully, I limped back towards the bedroom and there, not hidden, but hanging on the handle of the bedroom door was Ruth's brown handbag. I limped on into the bedroom carrying the handbag, intending to pick up and carry the travelling case over to my home, but instead of doing that I sat on the edge of the bed and my mind went blank — quite blank.

'Molly! Molly!' Ralph's voice brought me back to reality and once more I saw him standing in the doorway, dishevelled and showing signs of exhaustion. He was holding Ruth's wristwatch and her half-filled medicine bottle.

'For God's sake,' he said, *'Get up!* You must be brave.'

'I can't move, Ralph!' I whispered, 'I am too frightened, too scared.'

'I know — I know,' he said, 'I understand, I'm frightened too. I am very frightened.'

He sat beside me on the old-fashioned, very high bed and neither of us being tall, our feet dangled not quite touching the floor.

'Ralph,' I asked, pleadingly, 'Is this a nightmare? Tell me that it is. This can't be true . . .'

He shook his head, whispering, 'It is true. We are both here — and awake. No nightmare could be as dreadful as all this.'

Noticing the handbag I was still clutching, he took it from me. He opened it and taking out a bulging red plastic wallet he whispered, miserably, 'Just look! All this money. Poor unhappy woman, how she scrimped and saved.' He let the wallet fall to the floor, then, thrusting the medicine bottle and the wristwatch into the bulky, shabby handbag, he snapped it shut. Standing, he picked up the suitcase and left the room saying, urgently, 'Molly, for Christ's sake, pull yourself together. *Come and help me.'*

I could not help him. This time I stretched out on the bed, and I must have lost consciousness because I remember opening my eyes and feeling as though I had been asleep for some time. My breathing was shallow. I recalled, dreamily, of having once read in a magazine that if one breathed in deeply and slowly one would become relaxed, refreshed. I began to breathe deeply, slowly.

It worked, but oh how far away and high up it made the ceiling appear. The shabby ceiling was painted a bright blue. Ruth had been furious with Ralph when he had painted it. I remembered his gentle apology, of, 'I'm sorry, Ruthie, I thought that you would like it! Thought that it would be like sleeping beneath the sky.'

Beneath the sky? John's garden out there beneath the sky! I remembered that gaping black hole, waiting out in the garden to be filled in and the urgency of filling in the hole took complete possession of my mind. The hole was no longer a grave . . .

Tonight, when it became dark, Ralph would take Ruth's body away somewhere. Perhaps he would hide it on the vacant allotment? Perhaps . . .?

No matter what happened, that deep trench would give rise to leading questions from John, Jodie, Rob and from the police and from Ralph too.

Yes, *Ralph!* How was I to explain that monstrous hole to Ralph Moyston? He must never know that I had made such vile plans. I would prefer to die rather than to have Ralph, have anyone, know that I could have harboured such criminal intentions. My future would become unbearable. My future?

The future? The future could take care of itself. The enormity of the present flooded into my mind, striking hard, as cold sanity returned and with it such remorse, such guilt, that I cried out, 'God Almighty — what have I done? What am I allowing poor Ralph to do?'

It was not too late! We would bring Ruth back inside. Unpack her things. Call the police, explain to the police. I would be shamefully involved, but not accused of murder for I had righteously protected myself. Self-defence! It had been self-defence.

I crawled across the Moystons' backyard. Crawling was less painful than limping on my swollen ankle, and when I reached the low dividing fence, I stood up and leaned on it to see that Ralph was stamping the earth flat about the roots of John's precious, replanted camellia bushes. He, Ralph, had filled in the hideous hole and he waved a distracted hand toward me as without ceasing the wild stamping movements, he called, urgently, 'Molly, come and help me. You must help. Hose the grass. Get rid of this soil, this rubble.' He gestured wildly, hopelessly.

Slumped against the fence, I was unable to move or speak but I was able to think and my thoughts burnt and scalded and left scars which in turn burnt and scalded.

What had he done with Ruth's body? 'Into your house!' he had said. 'We'll hide her in your house!' he had said.

'Ralph,' I called, 'Ralph?' But he ignored me and worked on and he worked with the same unnatural energy that I had dug with earlier on.

As he worked he called, 'I've buried it as you intended doing.'

'No, no, no!' I cried, 'No, no, no.'

Continuing his stamping movements, he called, shouting loudly, 'Don't lie! Molly, you were going to do what I have done. You were not intending to call the police.'

'I was, I was . . .' My voice was high, shrill, 'Ralph, I *was* going to call them.'

He ran towards me, he fell, arose and ran again. He caught my hands, crushing them against his soiled shirt front and fear seemed to bleed from his eyes as he whispered, harshly, 'Where is she? Tell me, you must tell me. Now, at once!'

'What? I stammered. 'But you . . .' wrenching one hand free from his grip I gestured towards the chaos of John's garden where Ruth lay buried.

Ralph, ignoring my gesture, caught and captured my

hand again, whispering, 'Where *is* she? I must talk with her. I must . . .'

Oh, God, I thought, he has lost his reason.

His voice ground out, 'Tell me! She, *Jodie*, where is she? She killed Ruth! She killed her mother. I knew it all along. I —'

'No,' I said. 'No, you are wrong.'

'You lie! Don't lie! You are lying.'

'I am not lying. It was as I told you. I pushed her, she fell.' I struggled to free my hands but he clung even more and I saw that he was realizing his mistake.

'Jesus — Jesus!' Letting go of my hands Ralph burst into a paroxysm of wild weeping and I realized that he must have fully believed that his adored daugther had killed her mother and that if he had not thought so he would not have acted as he had.

'Ralph,' I spoke despairingly, 'So now we must act quickly. We must get Ruth back into your house. It will be awful, shocking, but we must and then we'll call the police. I shall call them. I came to tell you that. I'm sane now, Ralph. I came out to tell you. I'm sane now, Ralph.'

'Impossible. Impossible! We have gone too far. God help me, I am now as involved as you, and . . .'

'No,' I said, 'It needn't be like that.' I shook his arm roughly, 'Ralph, I shall tell the truth. Exactly as it happened. All but about the hole, and . . .'

'It's too late, Molly.' He was now weeping quietly, unashamedly, 'It's too late. By the time we dug her up, cleaned her up, and,' he began to shiver violently, 'Molly, Jodie and Rob could walk in on us in the middle of every-thing.'

'I know,' I interrupted, 'I know that but we must risk it. Ralph . . .'

I called to him in panic, for he was walking, shoulders bent, towards my back door. With great difficulty and in

23

pain I struggled over the low fence and stumbled my way into the house behind him. Ralph sat slumped in a chair, beside the kitchen table, with his face buried in his soil-covered hands.

'Ralph,' I began frantically, 'I repeat, I have been out of my mind, all day. Insane from fear. I admit my insanity, my cowardice, my *fear*.'

I might just as well have spoken to the chair. He was not listening at all and I realized that Ralph was at the end of his tether. With all my heart I wished that he had not returned home, not walked in to become so shockingly involved.

Why had he returned home from work? 'Ralph,' I questioned, 'Why did you return home? Ralph? *Ralph*?'

I repeated my question. At last he answered, saying, 'Last night, and this morning too, Ruth behaved like a mad woman. Lately she has been more upset, more violent than ever. Haven't you noticed?'

'Yes. Yes, I have!' I said. 'Lately there has been nothing but noise, beatings, punishments, in that home of yours.'

'Yes, it has been cruel, disgusting, so much so that I felt that we couldn't take it any more, and this morning as Ruth ranted on I told her that I had come to the end of my tether. Told her to stop making such a hellhole of our home, or else to pack up and get out. She screamed back that it would suit her down to the ground to clear out, go away, make a life for herself . . .'

'But she's always saying that. She has always said that.'

'I know, I *know*, but this morning *I* said it, and after I got to work I became upset, very upset, knowing that she would take it out on the kids. I telephoned several times but the phone just rang and rang. Somehow, I had an intuitive feeling that an awful thing had happened. I couldn't stand it. I came home.'

'Awful?' I said dully, 'Like . . .?'

'Like Rob or Jodie retaliating, especially Jodie, for recently she has been standing up to Ruth, and . . .' He sighed, tremulously, as an exhausted child sighs, and again he buried his face in his hands.

I sat opposite him on John's chair, in the nice yellow and white kitchen that John and I sat in every morning as we ate breakfast, read the morning paper and chatted about anything that came into our minds. I glanced at the electric clock on the wall. It was already a quarter past three!

'Ralph . . .' I spoke slowly and succinctly, 'Ralph, when everything that has happened is discovered. When that happens, Ralph . . .'

Ralph gazed at me, his eyes red and swollen. 'I mean,' I explained, 'Will you be able to cover up the fact that you left work, came home?'

He continued to stare at me uncomprehendingly but I spoke on, very carefully, very clearly, saying, 'Ralph, it will be best all around — for Jodie and Rob — that you are not involved in any way. You must not be involved. You must go home now, shower, change your clothes, return to the city, come home this evening just as though it had been a normal day.'

I continued to talk on and on until finally, but with no energy, no spirit, with no hope, Ralph went back to his own house.

After he had left, I sat awhile shivering and trembling, then I went out into John's garden and the world about me was radiant, the sky brilliantly blue. I limped over to the camellia hillock. Had I really uprooted John's camellia bushes?

Yes. The grass was dark with damp soil, littered with stones, debris. John took such pride in those camellia bushes. Soon, I realized, they would be uprooted again. But not by me. I was finished. Let the police do it. Meanwhile I would hose and rake the lawn.

I did all that, then I limped once more into the Moystons' house. Ralph was not there. I went into the front bedroom. I smoothed the bed cover, plumped up the pillows. I made a

25

neat pile of the books, putting them out of the way, beside the wardrobe. I went to the kitchen to clear up the broken drinking glass but Ralph had already done that, just as he had cleaned up the blood-stained tiles.

I went into the Moystons' bathroom. I saw that Ralph had used the shower and that he had carelessly left his earth-soiled shirt lying on the floor. I made the bathroom presentable and taking his soiled garment with me I left the Moystons' house.

Locking the kitchen door and placing the key in Ruth's usual hiding place, I went home.

I fixed things in my own house, then — I broke down. It was a short-lived, concentrated breakdown and during that period I seemed to stand apart, looking at myself, seeing myself as the pitiful creature that fear had turned me into.

I accepted the fact that life as I had known it was over. Shamefully, I knew that I was not courageous enough to admit to what I had done until circumstances forced me to do so.

I hoped fervently that everything would be over and done with before John returned home. And most of all I hoped that I would be given strength to go through the coming ordeal with at least a show of dignity.

Later on, when Jodie came over to ask me if I knew where her mother was, I was bathed and dressed, my hair was neat and I had used lipstick. My injured ankle was bandaged, resting on a stool.

'Hello, Jodie,' I said, 'I suppose Ruth has sent you to collect the bread,' and I looked at the girl, stretching my lips, showing my teeth. Jodie, I suppose, had thought that I was smiling at her.

CHAPTER TWO

W HEN A MAN AND A WOMAN have lived together in a small cottage for twenty-odd years it is reasonable to believe that they know each other intimately.

Molly and I married early, and the years following our marriage were passive, uneventful. I had no talent for business, for money-making but we were satisfied with our way of life. We lived within our means, managing to save enough to have a vacation every year. Perhaps our life together and our characters can be explained briefly, by recounting that on our first vacation we went to a modest hotel in a mountain resort, where the tariff was cheap, the food uninteresting but plentiful, and, liking the place well enough, we returned to it every time vacation came around again.

Our way of life was quiet, but pleasant. Then, about three years ago it began to change. One evening I returned home after a short business trip. We always used the term 'business trip' but actually, once every two months I accompanied my boss, Andrew Palmer, on *his* business trip, seeing to it that the samples of plastic materials he dealt in were packed in the correct cases and checking that his car was in good order to travel the long distances we covered. I acted as his chauffeur and clerk.

Returning to the city I was eager and anxious to get home, back to peace and order. Palmer is a tough insensitive man from whom I was forced to take any number of insults in order to keep my job. Molly's quiet attentiveness smoothed away these indignities.

A storm was raging, rain fell in a deluge and as I hurried

from the bus stop I worried about my garden — heavy rains always washed away so much of the precious topsoil — and I fretted about a leak in the kitchen roof that needed mending. I wished that we were better off so that I could afford professional tradesmen for odd jobs and devote all my spare time to the garden, make it the place of beauty I wanted it to be. I had wondered whether I could ask Molly to forgo our mountain holiday and spend the money and the time on the garden, then I thought of her indifference to gardening and decided it was hardly a fair request.

Passing by the large, vacant section that adjoined our property, I wished again that our house had been included in the real estate deal a few years back, when the land had been purchased for the building of an apartment block. We had no luck, I thought, no luck at all, really. But as I entered my front gate I suddenly felt quite fortunate and glad to be home.

I have always been relieved that Molly is never nervous whilst I am away. It was I, not Molly, who reacted nervously when our home was robbed. I was also damned annoyed at losing the recently purchased television, radio and record player which I had not bothered to insure against theft.

I knew from years of similar reunions that Molly would be in the kitchen. That the table would be nicely set for dinner. I knew that we would eat lamb cutlets — it was Wednesday — I knew that on opening the front door, I would take off my raincoat and call, 'Molly, I'm home, dear!' and that she would come into the hall, wearing a crisp apron with her hair neatly groomed, smiling, saying, 'Hello, John dear. So — you're home!'

'Yes,' I would answer, 'I'm home,' and I would kiss her cheek and she would kiss the air or perhaps her kiss would land on my ear.

But that evening — three years ago — when I stood in the hall calling, 'Molly, I'm home,' although I was not then aware of it, the pattern of our lives changed, for instead of

28

coming into the hall, Molly called to me from the living room, saying, 'John, in here! John! I'm in the living room.'

I went into the living room. Molly sat on a stiff-backed chair with her left leg resting on a stool, and the ankle was bandaged.

Concerned, I was about to ask her what had happened, when a man — a stranger — sitting on another stiff-backed chair, got to his feet and spoke to me, introducing himself as Grey and explaining that he belonged to a branch of the police force which made enquiries about missing persons.

'Missing persons?' I looked at Molly. Molly was home. I was home.

'Who is missing?' I asked.

Molly and the detective evidently expected the other to answer. A short silence ensued, then Grey informed me that our neighbour, Ruth Moyston, had presumably left her home two days before, and that, so far, no one knew of her whereabouts. Her husband, Ralph Moyston, had been upset about his wife going away without a word to anyone, but he, Moyston, had not become deeply alarmed until that afternoon and he had notified the police.

Grey explained that he was in our home, questioning us, because he had been told that my wife and Mrs Moyston were friends, and of course, because we were not only the Moystons' closest, but their only neighbours.

'That's correct!' I said and I added, 'My goodness!' I sat down and took out my pipe. I was intrigued because nothing quite as dramatic as this had happened to us before. 'My goodness,' I repeated, 'What can have happened to her?'

'Why do you say that?' asked Grey.

'I beg your pardon — say what?'

'Surmise that something has happened to Mrs Moyston? So far, her husband, her children and your wife, have all been asking, "Where can she have gone?" '

'Oh,' I interrupted, 'I meant that too. Ruth is such a loner,

29

and certainly, although she's forever yelling that she intends to take off and leave Ralph and the kids, I have never known her to be away from home for one night, let alone two.'

I was becoming more interested, quite enthusiastic, and Grey was becoming quite animated in his manner and expression as he took a notebook from one of his pockets, saying, 'Never?'

'What?' I asked, 'Never . . . what?'

'Mrs Moyston has *never* been away from her home overnight?'

'So far as I know, and except for my business trips and holidays I am always at home in the evenings, and I assure you I should know, for Ruth — Mrs Moyston — is a loud-mouthed, noisy woman.' I stuffed tobacco into my pipe, lit a match to it and puffed away.

Grey lost his animation, saying flatly, 'Mr Blake, if you're away so much I can't accept your statement, or take it seriously.'

The man plainly thought I was a fool. He turned from me to Molly and by his manner I gathered that he had already asked her many questions.

'And so, Mrs Blake,' he said, 'You can think of nothing unusual at all? You're quite certain then, that nothing unusual occurred? I mean, could, for instance, Mrs Moyston have received a letter, a telephone call that upset her in any way? Perhaps . . .'

'Not that I know of,' interrupted Molly. 'Everything was as usual. On Sunday — the day before she left home — Ruth did her weekly wash, she polished the kitchen tiles, then, she came over here. We had coffee together, she chatted, talked as usual, of usual things, then she went back home and . . .'

'Does Mrs Moyston always do her weekly wash on Sunday?' Mr Grey interrupted.

'Yes,' said Molly, 'She does. Ruth likes her family to see

how difficult her life is. She is a hard woman, very stern. She never lets her children, especially her daughter, have much fun or freedom. Ralph, Mr Moyston, is gentle. He always lets her have her way...' Molly hesitated, '...I sometimes think Ralph is as scared of Ruth as the children are.'

'Scared?' queried Grey. 'Surely that's a rather strong word?'

'Ruth is a strong woman,' replied Molly firmly. 'Jodie and Rob have good reason to be scared of her moods. That doesn't mean that they don't love her, I am sure they *do*. As for me, yes, some of Ruth's ways do upset me. When I hear her yelling at the children or lashing out at Ralph with her tongue I dislike her intensely, but, for all that, she has her good qualities and we are friends...' Molly turned to me, saying, 'Wouldn't you say that Ruth and I are good friends, John?'

'Well,' I said, 'I never think of her as your good friend, but you are quite friendly. Personally,' I faced Grey — 'Personally, Mr Grey, I detest the woman. I would be glad never to set eyes on her again.'

'John!' interrupted Molly, admonishingly, 'How can you!'

Grey stood up, saying, 'Mr Blake, before I leave I would like a statement from you concerning the last time you saw Mrs Moyston.'

'A statement! That's ludicrous! I see very little of her, as little as I am able to.'

'Nevertheless, I require a statement,' he insisted. And so, I gave him a statement, saying that the last time I had seen and spoken to Ruth Moyston had been the Tuesday morning, a week before she left home.

'I was leaving on a business trip.' I stated, 'Ruth, Mrs Moyston, called to me from her front window —'

'Called to you? What exactly did she say?' Grey sounded ridiculously suspicious.

' "Goodbye, John!" That's all. She just called out, "Goodbye, John." '

'Was there a note of — let us say — a note of finality in her goodbye?'

'Certainly not! It was just an ordinary, everyday goodbye.'

'Well,' said Grey. 'Thank you, both. I'll be on my way.'

I went to the door with him, and after watching him walk down the path then enter the Moystons' house I hurried back to Molly. She was still sitting on the stiff-backed chair, and kissing her smooth cheek, I said with some concern, 'Now, tell me! Your leg? What happened? What is wrong with your leg?'

'It's my ankle,' she explained. 'I slipped in the shower. It's very painful —'

'*Shower*?' I interrupted. 'You seldom shower! You love your bath tub. What were you doing under the shower?'

For the first time ever, my wife spoke to me waspishly, obviously strained by the events of the last few days, 'I-was-taking-a shower, John,' she said, 'Can't I take a shower without you making a drama of the fact?'

'Molly,' I placated, 'I'm sorry, dear. That detective fellow *has* upset us. My goodness, isn't it queer? About Ruth, I mean! Where can she have gone? Is Ralph greatly upset? I had better go over and see him, poor chap, and how about the kids? I bet they're glad that the old girl has skedaddled . . .'

'John,' Molly interrupted whisperingly, 'I'm sorry dinner is not ready. I feel very off-colour. There are lamb chops, there is a cold baked custard. John, I must lie down. I must rest. I'm sorry . . .'

Accepting my help, she limped into our bedroom. I went into the kitchen and ignoring the lamb chops and the custard, I made some toast and coffee, then, after eating it on the hoof, I carried a snack-tray into Molly. She was lying on the bed, obviously asleep, but still fully clad.

Feeling at a loss — also rather neglected — I tidied up the kitchen then, concerned at the havoc the rain would be causing in my back garden, I was about to put on my old raincoat, take up my flashlight to go and investigate, when the front door bell rang.

It was the detective Grey again. Ralph Moyston stood behind him and behind Ralph were Jodie and Rob. They all trooped into the living room where Grey at once made a speech, saying, 'I have just been informed that Mrs Moyston has taken away a certain amount of clothing and personal possessions, also quite a large sum of money. This causes one to believe that she has indeed left home, intending to stay away for some time.'

He looked up at the ceiling. My gaze followed his and I noticed that the paint was flaking a little, then he continued on, still with his gaze fixed on the ceiling, saying, ' . . .But, I am not at all *satisfied*.'

Resembling a darting bird his glance swooped from the ceiling to our faces, causing me — at least — to squirm uneasily and feel that I knew something, and was deliberately withholding information from him.

Jodie began to sniffle and Ralph drew the girl to his side, saying, 'Now then, don't cry, pet.'

Ignoring this tender interlude between father and daughter, Grey continued briskly, saying, 'From all accounts Mrs Moyston is a careful, a methodical woman. Would this careful and methodical woman — without a word to anyone — leave her home, leave the house she has so devotedly cared for over the years — lock the back door — place the key in its hiding place and yet leave most windows in the house wide open —'

'Wide open? The windows left wide open?' interrupted Ralph, 'After the recent robberies? No, Ruth would never do that, and as a matter of fact, Mr Grey, you are mistaken. When I came home that evening, all the windows were closed.'

'Your daughter had closed them.' Mr Grey turned to Jodie, saying politely, 'Miss Moyston, I would like you to tell me — once more — exactly how things were when you returned home from school on Monday.'

Jodie, unaccustomed to such formal address, blushed wildly. I smiled at her. 'Go ahead, Jo,' encouraged Ralph, tenderly.

Jodie went ahead, in the rapid, but halting, manner peculiar to teenagers, saying, 'I came home as usual and as usual the windows were open. The kitchen door was locked — that wasn't usual — I knocked on the door and called out because I knew Mum must be home. But she wasn't home, so I looked and found the key and I went inside and then I came over here, to Aunty Molly, because I thought Mum would be here — and I was rather glad of that — because Mum had been — well — she had been a bit upset with me before I left for school and I was glad that I'd see her first together with Aunty Molly, not by herself. But she wasn't here. Aunty Molly said she thought that Mum must be out, because earlier on in the day the baker-boy had told her, Aunty Molly, that Mum had not answered him. Then Aunty Molly told me that she — Aunty Molly, I mean — had sprained her ankle during the day and that after her accident she'd yelled out to Mum to come over and help her bandage it but Mum hadn't answered. Then, when Rob came home from school, he came over here too, and we all talked and thought it was a bit . . . funny.'

'Funny?' Mr Grey interrupted Jodie's soliloquy.

'Yes, funny,' repeated Jodie, 'Like . . . strange, unusual! Anyway, I made a cup of tea for Aunty Molly and Rob went home and it was *Rob* who closed the windows, because it was getting windy — real stormy and rainy — and then he started on his homework for school. And then when I went home a bit later I got a jolt when I found out that Mum had taken Dad's old case and that she'd also taken a lot of other things too. When Dad came in, we told him and he couldn't believe us and he went right through the house and he found out what we had said was all true and he said Mum must be playing a trick — to tease us — and that — for sure — she'd be home soon. But she hasn't come home, even yet . . .?'

Jodie threw herself into Ralph's arms and wept noisily. 'Mummy, Mummy . . .' she sobbed and I thought of the nagging, harsh treatment Ruth had so often meted out to her daughter and I wondered at the loyalties of family ties and relationships.

'Mr Grey, my daughter is very upset,' said Ralph. 'May she go home now?'

'No.' Grey turned to me, saying, 'Mr Blake, ask Mrs Blake to come in here, please.'

'She is asleep,' I protested. 'Is it really necessary to disturb her? Wouldn't the morning do?'

Grey declared that the morning would not do and so I went to call Molly, who, presumably disturbed and deeply perturbed by Jodie's violent sobbing fit, was standing in the hall, looking so ill that I was sure she was about to faint. I placed an arm about her, saying, 'There's no bad news, dear! Jodie's just upset! Blast Grey and his overbearing officiousness. It's too bad of him but he insists on seeing you again.' I stood by, admiringly, as she managed to gain control of herself before entering the living room.

Jodie, tear-stained and shaking, rushed to Molly, who held her close, and Grey, slightly abashed, said, 'Mrs Blake, I am sorry to disturb you again but why — when I questioned you previously — did you not tell me that Mrs Moyston had taken clothing and other things away with her?'

'I thought you already knew,' said Molly, flatly, 'I thought that Ralph would have told you.'

'Mr Moyston did not tell me. I have just discovered the

facts,' said Grey. 'Now, Mrs Blake, on Monday, didn't *you* think it unusual that Mrs Moyston should have gone out leaving the windows open?'

'No, for I was not sure that Ruth *had* gone out,' explained Molly. 'Monday was a difficult day for me, I had injured my ankle, and I was in pain. When I called to Ruth, I suppose I must have noticed that the windows were open, and now I do remember that the bread delivery boy mentioned the fact. I'm sorry, Mr Grey, but I'm afraid I'm rather a coward and pain upsets me.'

She had smiled in a self-deprecating manner and I had sighed with relief, knowing that the pain in her ankle accounted for her out-of-character behaviour. It was true that she could not take pain. A visit to the dentist was, to Molly, like a condemned criminal's walk to the execution chamber.

Grey stayed on for awhile, questioning and writing down the scraps of information we gave him about Ruth, and before taking his leave, he told Ralph that he would be in touch. He admonished us all to do all that we could to assist in the search for Ruth Moyston.

The three Moystons lingered on for some time and I was heartily pleased when they trailed off back to their own home. I was concerned about Molly, and against her wishes I insisted on bathing her cruelly swollen ankle, and then bandaging it tightly. Gradually, she seemed to relax and I smiled, saying, 'There now! It will soon be better. Poor girl! Poor dear!'

Suddenly her eyes were suffused with tears and taking my hand in hers she whispered, 'John — John, I am filled with shame — I am such a *coward*, John . . .'

About to refute her poor opinion of herself I was prevented by Ralph who entered our living room carrying a bottle of Napoleon brandy, saying tentatively, 'John, I thought a drop of this might be helpful to Molly. Help her to relax, and ease her pain.'

I was just about dead on my feet but Ralph appeared so lost, so woebegone that I replied cheerfully, 'Very thoughtful of you, Ralph, and not only for Molly, eh . . .?' Feeling quite bucked up, I brought drinking glasses. There are few things I like more than a tot of good cognac.

During the past three years enquiries have been made, various members of the police have called and questioned us, but so far, to no avail. Ruth Moyston has not returned home, and Ralph has taken it in his stride, quite as though to have one's wife disappear into thin air — so to speak — is not at all very much out of the ordinary. He is certain that she will return home one of these days. Jodie and Rob have left school and have undistinguished jobs. To hear them speak of their mother one must believe that Ruth — quite contrary to fact — had been a tender, caring parent. Rob and Jodie are healthier and certainly more self confident these days.

Although Molly's ankle mended, it has left her with a dragging limp and she has grown vague in some ways, and neglectful of her appearance and of the house. I know she is sensitive about her limp, feeling that it is a disfigurement, which is nonsensical. But nothing I say or do comforts her or changes her mind.

Rather to my astonishment, she has become quite a gardener. All her time, all the money we once used for holiday trips, for visits to theatres, small gifts to relatives and friends at Christmas time, that money has been spent on 'garden improvement'.

The lawns are emerald green, their borders meticulously straight. Exotic plants and seasonal flowers bloom luxuriantly, profusely, but never is one cut and brought into the house.

When I first noticed Molly's interest in gardening I had been delighted, but then it seemed to develop into what I can only describe as an obsession. At the same time she became moody, and for the first time in our marriage we had arguments, with me begging her to see a psychiatrist and Molly refusing, saying wearily, 'Leave me alone, John. Please leave me alone! All I want is to be left alone and left to my gardening. Is *that* asking too much of life?'

'No, not at all, dear,' I had soothed, 'By all means, Molly, garden away to your heart's content, but let us share the work and the pleasure. You know how I enjoy gardening, and . . .'

'Right!' she exclaimed. 'John, you take over the front garden. That's fair! You have the front and I'll have the back.'

I laughed, saying that we were not children. That adults — especially a husband and a wife — surely did not have to share out gardens like pieces of candy.

It was no use and for peace at any price I began to care for the small front yard, but my heart had always been in the spacious back garden that I had landscaped, built up from the uncultivated rough land it had been twenty years before. I could not raise any enthusiasm towards the front garden and as time went by, I gave up all interest in gardening *per se*. I also lost interest in the house, and from the street our once immaculate home presents a rather sorry spectacle. Weeds choke the garden beds and the grass grows tall, neglected and scraggy. Paint is needed on the house and the front steps are cracked, a hinge is missing on the gate.

Molly, although extremely reticent, had always responded tentatively, but warmly, to my love-making. Naturally, when she was in pain from her injured ankle I made no advances and then when she complained, saying that she was suffering from insomnia, out of consideration for her I moved myself and my belongings into the spare bedroom. The room that we had shyly and hopefully alluded to as 'the nursery' during the first five or six years of our marriage.

Along with the years it has become known as the spare

room and in that room I spend many sleepless hours, worrying about the unhappy changes in our home and in our lives. However I am rather relieved to be on my own. Being near Molly distresses me, for I cannot understand her and things that I don't understand upset me.

Several times, no, more than several times, during the night, I have heard Molly crying. The first time, I hurried to her and attempted to comfort her, whispering that I loved and desired her, but she pushed me away just as she pushes me away from every moment in her life.

I knew that my wife needed professional care. I knew that I should do something about it, but I kept putting it off and away from my thoughts, always hoping, always expecting that every evening, when I returned home, I would be greeted by the placid, happy wife I had so respected and admired.

There were times when I quite envied Ralph Moyston his freedom. However, he seemed to spend much of his time searching the city, looking for Ruth. He would return home on Saturdays and Sundays, full of his explorations, and he would come to our home to talk, for Jodie and Rob were usually out on dates.

I was quite pleased to have him call in and I would put down my novel or newspaper, glad of the interruption, 'No luck, Ralph?' I would ask, politely.

Molly would merely glance up from her beloved seed catalogues, then lose herself in them again.

It was as always — no luck — and after allowing me time to 'tut tut' and be sympathetic, Ralph would tell me of the places in the city that he had visited that day. He went everywhere, he told me. He went to the zoo, to the botanic gardens, to the museum, to the art galleries, to cinemas — always looking for Ruth.

He frequented small coffee shops, and he got to know the girls who served him and he would tell me stories of these girls' lives, and stories about countless other people that he sat beside in parks, on bus seats, everywhere and any-where.

He showed people Ruth's photograph. He carried her photograph in his wallet. 'One day,' Ralph said with quiet confidence, 'One day, John, I just know that someone is going to say they have seen Ruth. That they know where she is.'

The fact that Ruth might have gone off to a distant country town, or even abroad, never seemed to enter his mind, and the thought that perhaps Ruth was dead and gone, I felt sure, never entered his mind either.

Truthfully speaking, I seldom thought of Ruth Moyston. I had never liked her, and although I was as mystified as anyone by her disappearance and certainly hoped that she was alive and well, I rather hoped that she would never turn up, for one difficult woman in such close proximity was quite enough for any man.

I settled down to the routine of day following day, believing that the sameness would continue; which it did, until the real estate speculator who owned the adjoining vacant lot, came to call.

At last, he said, he saw his way clear for his company to begin construction of a high-rise apartment building and he wanted to purchase my property and the Moystons' as well.

The price he offered was excellent. New vistas opened up. I would now be able to care properly for Molly, have a really excellent doctor advise us. We would move to a new environment, an apartment, somewhere on the waterfront — no garden — Molly and I would take up fishing, sail-ing . . .

CHAPTER THREE

B EFORE LEAVING HOME this morning John had looked at me with an expression of scorn. He spoke to me harshly and bitterly. 'Molly,' he said, 'You have become a destructive woman! Do you realize that? Are you aware that you have developed an unhealthy, a ludicrous power complex?'

It is dreadful to have John despise me. If he knew the truth he would realize how mistaken his opinion of me is, for I am bent only on preservation, and I am not powerful. I resemble a mouse crouching between the claws of a well-fed cat, awaiting the moment that the cat will feel the pangs of hunger.

Last night it was as though the claws of the cat pressed in on me and pricked my skin, drew a little blood.

Ralph Moyston, Jodie, Rob and John, all filled with excitement and with a dozen and varied happy plans for their futures, had gathered together in our living room. Money at last! Quite a lot of money! Our two houses were to be sold, pulled down. Jodie wanted to call Bill — her steady boyfriend — tell him that Ralph had promised her a sizeable amount of money to purchase a piece of land and that they, Jodie and her young man, could be married much earlier than they had planned.

'Call him now, Jo,' Rob advised, 'call him now.'

I looked up from my book on *Plants and their Diseases*, and speaking for the first time, I said calmly and coldly, 'Don't call Bill, Jodie, I am not selling this property and if they can't purchase this one right next door to their land, they

41

will not want to buy your parents' home. Just forget about it.'

John finally broke the silence that followed my statement, saying, 'What are you saying, Molly?' He was startled and quite aghast.

'I think you heard me loud and clear,' I replied without looking up as I firmly underlined a paragraph in my book. 'I've no intention of selling the house. I have lived here for many years. It's all I want — or need.'

'She's joking, or out of her mind!' cried Rob. 'Aunty Molly, you must be kidding! Think of the money! You can have a much nicer house. You —'

'You wouldn't be so cruel, so selfish,' cried Jodie. 'No one could!'

Ralph made no comment. I glanced up and saw the regretful expression on his face and I flashed my eyes back to the blur of the printed page of my book.

Never, not once, since that now far-off dreadful day, have Ralph Moyston and I been alone together. Not once have we mentioned that which lies beneath John's camellia bushes.

In many ways I admire Ralph and I depend on him. He is standing up to the stress and strain more courageously than I. It is always easier for me when he is at home . . . nearby . . . for Ralph knows everything. Only he and I know why it is impossible for me to leave the house, the garden that I hate with a violence that poisons every moment of my waking hours and that fills with nightmare the few restless periods of sleep I get.

Of course, Ralph could not come out openly on my side, for he is implicated too, quite dangerously so. I could not bear to look at him again, and so, without raising my eyes, I murmured, 'You don't want to sell, or do you, Ralph?'

Ralph replied gently, 'For myself — no — not really. It would only be for Jodie and Rob. For myself — one way or the other — I don't mind . . .'

'I mind,' John expostulated harshly, 'This property belongs to me, I bought it with money that I have slaved for over the years. It is the only thing in the world that I own, and now, at last, it is going to pay dividends. What you do, Ralph, depends on you. I am selling. That is definite.'

'Wow-ee!' Like a gust of wind Jodie rushed over to John and began to hug and kiss him and Rob began to explain to Ralph that, if he could buy a truck — he knew exactly the one he wanted — he would give up his clerking job and go into business for himself.

John was filling his pipe and his hands shook with nervous tension. I loved him dearly, my heart ached for him, but my voice was cold, as I said, 'It's no use talking about buying a truck, Rob. The cold fact is that people can only sell that which belongs to them and this house belongs to me. This property is legally in my name. It belongs to Mary Heather Blake, and I am not selling it . . .'

The evening had been a dreadful one — especially for John — and this morning, as I watched him trudging along towards the bus stop I wept bitterly. Then, after he had turned the corner I walked briskly through the house — I never drag my leg when alone — and I noticed that John had not washed up his breakfast dishes as has become his habit, and that he had not finished drinking his much loved coffee.

I felt the coffee pot, it was still hot so I poured myself a mug of coffee and carried it out to my garden. I intended to begin building up about the camellia bushes, for the ground has sunk again, quite a bit. Over the years I had harvested loads of rock and soil from the vacant land beside us. Now I am concerned knowing that soon that supply route will be lost to me.

How were my weeds coming along? Not a weed to be seen! I have bad luck with weeds. Everything flourishes in my garden, except weeds, and yes, in a way, the camellias, for although the bushes are sturdy and covered with glistening leaves, no flowers ever come into bloom. Always when the seasons for camellia flowers arrive I arise at dawn every day, and going to the garden, I pinch off the small, hard buds. I am fanatical about the matter. Never, never, could I endure seeing flowers bloom on *those* bushes.

This morning, after loading my hand-cart with rocks, I trundled it across the lawn, pleased to see how the wheels scarred and tore at the grass. Later on I will be able to fill in time by attending to the damage I was intentionally causing. Sometimes, to create work for myself, I perform remarkable acts of vandalism. I wish that the garden were twice its size.

I have decided to break up the present rock-garden, completely, and build it again from scratch. It will take some time. A week? Ten days maybe? Or, if I remember to go slowly, even longer.

I like working in this spot, by the rock-garden, because here I can talk to Ruth. She and I had never been close, not really, for it had been she who had always done the talking, telling me of her troubles and airing her complaints. I, not having had troubles in those far-off days, or any complaints to make, had no need to talk, but, now, ah, these days *I* have all the troubles and I am full of complaints and Ruth hears them all.

This morning I told her how I had witnessed the breaking up of a man's dreams, of how I had torn away every shred of pride and hope that John possessed.

When I had dropped the bombshell, about my owning and not being willing to sell our property, John had eventually cried out, half laughingly, 'Hey, hey, hold everything! Certainly the house was put solely in your name, Molly, because, and *only because*, I care for you. Because with the house legally in your name and if I died before you, then you would be left better off.'

John had continued on, at first calmly, then angrily, then

44

furiously. Then with great kindness, then, like a beggar, he implored me to give in, to change my mind.

I sat listening to him, my face expressionless, but every word he spoke cut deep. Finally, I replied calmly, saying, 'John, the law is the law. The house is legally in my name. I am not stupid. I know as well as you do how it *came* into my possession. Why go on about it? I will never part with it. Please stop worrying and pestering me.'

Then I had picked up my flashlight, put on my old cardigan and I had gone out into the dark garden to begin my usual nightly snail hunt.

John had not followed me, and this morning, just before he left, he said, 'Molly, for the love of God, won't you change your mind about selling the house?'

'No John,' I said, and he called me destructive. I went into my bedroom and shut the door. Then I came out and watched him walking away, along the street, and he looked so despondent, so tired, and I loved him so dearly that my heart felt as though it was about to burst open.

And about Jodie, Ruth! That hysterical scene she put on! Yes, your daughter, Jodie, all her dreams went bust, because of me. And Rob — Ruth, it was pathetic to watch Rob's nice, but always twitching, face as he saw his dreams fade. Ralph, well, he played his part as I had played mine.

Ruth, Ralph keeps away from me just as I keep away from him. You might think that our guilt — my guilt, that is — and his knowledge of it, should draw us together, but that is not so.

Ralph has become a little strange, Ruth, and in all the world no one knows why, but I. I know that he knows where you are because he put you here, but there are times when I think that he has forgotten. He appears so serious, so sincere about his searching for you, about expecting you to return home of your own volition.

When I hear him talking to John I am almost sure that he has forgotten, and that would mean of course, that he is losing his mind, but then, he will catch me looking at him, and I know that he remembers only too well. Ralph and I understand and sympathize with one another, but we do not talk about you . . . ever.

I can no longer recall the happiness, the simplicity, of life as it used to be. Yes, Ruth, even in death you are powerful and destructive. You take all human dignity from me, I have become your slave. It is incredibly horrifying to have become the slave of a corpse. I see no beauty anywhere. My gaze is focussed only and always on you. Food has lost all flavour. I am unable to sleep. I . . .

Ruth, everything is your fault! You were too harsh, too cruel. No one really cared when you, well — when you died. If Ralph had cared for you, really cared, it is most likely that I would have spent these past years in prison.

Ruth, I am beginning to wish, very much, that you had been nicer to Ralph and that he had called the police that day, but what is done is done.

Really Ruth, you have no idea how my attitudes, my ethics, have changed. Remember how you always revelled in newspaper reports of murders and how I could not bear to hear about them? Well, that has all changed and these days, I take a deep interest in them. I never want a criminal caught. When a murder is committed and no one is arrested for it, I feel as though I am not so unusual after all, and that most probably there are many cases such as ours. People disappear. The police make enquiries. The person is listed as missing, when, actually, like you — you are listed as missing, Ruth — they are dead. Dead — and buried . . .

I am always extremely pleased when one of the missing persons does turn up — alive, I mean. Whenever that happens, Jodie and Rob become excited and Ralph goes into his act of how he just knows that one of these days you are going to arrive at the front door. I used to be embarrassed by Ralph's artificial goings on but now I take little notice.

It is amazing the number of people that get away with murder, Ruth. In this very city of ours, during the past three years, I could tell of at least four very spectacular cases. Persons high up and quite important have been murdered, and no matter how arduously the police and the analysts and the detectives and the public have worked and tested and inquired and talked, these crimes have not — as yet — been solved. Never will be in all probability.

Ruth, I have a dread of the police. Several times during the past three years different policemen have come here. I have heard the door bell ring, gone to the door, and each time I have nearly passed out . . . cold. Big, tall, uniformed men standing there. I . . .

Oh, yes, I tell you, I have had some formidable shocks. It does not matter that those men were merely making enquiries, wanting to know if I kept a dog or a television set, and if so, did I have a licence? It just matters that for days after my nerves would be shot to pieces.

My life is dreadful. Every facet of my life is sad and dreadful.

Ruth, have I told you the news about Mr Grey? He has been promoted. He has become quite an important man. I read about his promotion in the newspaper. I am glad that he has ceased coming to see Ralph. It was shattering when he used to call. I believe, though, that Ralph still sees him occasionally, for Ralph was telling John only a few weeks back that Mr Grey is still interested in your disappearance.

Well, as long as he keeps away from here, that is all I ask. I wish him every success, I hope he really gets to the top of the tree and then his mind will be on higher and more important things than the disappearance of Ruth Moyston — of you.

Ruth, the camellia bushes are quite tall now. Remember when they were so small and how pleased John was when they had their first flowers? He was specially thrilled with the centre bush because of its pure white flowers. I like the

47

two pink ones best, but John always adored white flowers. That is why I grow so many — white flowers, I mean — but he does not notice flowers any more.

John has given up noticing, wanting other things too. I can't speak about that.

Sad, yes, everything is very sad in my life. My sister Madge died recently. I miss her so much, she was the only friend I had left. All my friends have given me away, or perhaps I gave them away? I don't quite know. Of course, I have given up going to church, and you know how I worked for the Ladies' Aid and how I loved Sundays and going to church.

I could not even bring myself to attend Madge's funeral service. John was profoundly shocked; he told me that I was peculiar. Peculiar! That was the word he used, and he was correct. I am peculiar, and as well as that I am weary from the strain of life and of the distress I cause John and . . .

Ruth! Ruth! Right now — at this moment — two cars are driving on to the land next to us. I see a group of men. They are getting out of the cars, strolling about, looking the place over and one of them is coming in our direction, he is putting his head over the fence. He is calling to me, asking if I am the owner, the one refusing to sell this place of ours.

Ruth, I am going to pretend that I am deaf as well as lame. From now on, I shall be hard of hearing. In a moment I will look up and pretend to see him for the first time and I will pretend to get a shock and when he speaks, I will look vacant and point to my ears.

He has gone now, Ruth. The man has gone back to join his mates. This business of building the apartments is, I fear, a calamity, a . . .

Calamity! What a terrifying word . . . And, oh dear God, what have I done? The rock-garden is a complete wreck — a shambles! I had not meant to upset it quite so much.

Never mind, it is all to the good. It means that I will be seriously, fully occupied for a few weeks at least. Ruth, it is midday, I am going in to have a cup of coffee, eat a hunk of cheese, and with all my heart, I wish you were alive and able to sit and have coffee with me.

CHAPTER FOUR

SINCE MOLLY'S REFUSAL to sell our home — home? property is a more suitable word — I spend as little time as possible in her company. Apart from my anger at her outrageous behaviour, it distresses me to see the woman she has become. What has caused this deterioration of my wife's personality? I am always trying to find a reason, any reason at all, but I remain puzzled.

I often think back to the time when we first met. It was just after World War II. I had not been accepted into the armed forces because although hale and hearty in every other respect, I had a back injury which, although cured later, was considered to be incurable at that time.

In some quarters I had been considered a coward, which naturally had caused me painful embarrassments, and also had prevented me from getting a good job, preference always being given to those young men who had bravely done their stint during the war years.

Molly was the first girl I ventured to date. She had been working as a sales girl in a department store, and her gentle manner, her obvious liking and admiration for me, not only soothed my inner hurts, but also bolstered my ego. Although our first date had consisted of a Sunday afternoon walk through the botanic gardens and tea and toast at the cafeteria there, she, Molly, seemed to enjoy every minute.

Our Sunday dates had continued and had graduated into regular Saturday evening dates as well. We would go to the movies, see a film, and always part with the unspoken of, but understood, Sunday date.

Once, we had gone to a live theatre and even now, twenty years later, that evening stands out in my memory. For months, I had put a little cash away each pay day towards the great event, about which Molly had known nothing. I had embarrassed myself and asked one of the fellows in the office if he would lend me his formal dinner suit. Rather unwillingly, he had agreed and perhaps sensing my embarrassment, he had told me that the suit actually belonged to a friend of his. 'For God's sake, John,' he had pleaded, 'Don't let anything happen to it.' I had promised, and indeed the evening was at times spoilt for me because of my worry about my friend's friend's suit.

When the cash box held enough for the theatre tickets — and for dinner in a good restaurant — I had asked Molly, seemingly casually, 'Care to have dinner, take in a stage-show next Friday?'

Her gasp of pleased excitement rewarded me as I had seldom been rewarded in life. However, I thought that her enthusiasm had waned a little at the mention of formal attire. 'Meet you on Friday, then,' I had said, adding as a parting shot, 'We'll dress formally! I have dress circle seats for us!'

'Oh,' she murmured rather uneasily, and when I asked her what was wrong she said, lightly, 'Nothing. Nothing at all! Everything's fine! I'll meet you at six-thirty, and John, I am so pleased and excited.'

We were married for some time before Molly confessed the agonies that *she* had gone through, borrowing a formal dress, a wrap and an evening bag, from various girl friends so that she could do the great occasion justice.

In some ways it had not been a completely enjoyable experience. Too much sacrifice had gone into the saving of the money. Molly and I were strangers to each other in our borrowed plumes, and both of us — unknown to the other — had been nervous of any mishap to them. But we enjoyed that show and we enjoyed the trip home, during

51

which we spoke of and argued, praised, criticized the play, and laughed as we never had before.

I kissed Molly that night, for the first time. She had responded, shyly, gladly, and I am sure she considered herself engaged to be married. I know that I felt manly, capable of anything, and one year later we were married. I admired my wife and relied on her. I liked everything about her. I believed that she felt as I did, in every way, and I fully believed that she always would.

As the chaos of building increases on the land adjoining our home I am relaxing a little, not fretting so much about her refusal to sell our property. Molly, I believe, will change her views of her own accord, for the noise, the action, the dust, make a continuous pandemonium.

'Molly won't be able to take it much longer,' I told Ralph, and he said he supposed that I was right and that it should be just a matter of time.

'Yes,' Ralph had agreed with me, 'It is much worse for Molly than for any of us. We are never here during the week days. She is the only one actually suffering because of the noise. Yes, John, be patient, time will do the trick.'

Three months have passed by and the huge building project has become a grotesque steel skeleton, dwarfing our small houses. The workmen now start very early every morning and to escape the noise I leave home an hour earlier than is necessary and I have taken to walking the three miles to the city and my health and my appetite are improving. This morning, however, I awoke with a headache, and feeling off colour I decided to wait and catch the bus. Preparing my breakfast of boiled eggs, toast and coffee, I groaned aloud at each metallic clang, at the screech of metal on metal, and at the general buzz and ear-shattering medley of construction going on. Looking out of the grimy kitchen window, I watched Molly, who stood, as though lost in a dream, with her arms folded, staring down at the really beautiful rock-garden she has recently been working on again, and as I watched, sounds of shocking confusion came from the building project, beginning with the high, terrified scream of a man and ending with the deafening crash of a steel girder as it fell from a height on to a pile of other girders lying on the ground.

There was an ugly beat of silence, then sounds of panic — men's voices yelling — and mixed in with all of that, work had started up again, the work of more than thirty men, many of them armed with electrical tools.

Later on, I found out that a workman had fallen, as well as the girder, and that he had been seriously injured.

When the chaos had quietened down, I placed my untouched cup of coffee on to the table, and going out into the garden, I called to Molly. Molly, during the entire period, had not moved. She had remained lost in contemplation of her much-loved rock-garden and even the sound of her own name, called close by, made no impression on her. When I touched her shoulder, she turned, gazing at me with startled, fear-filled eyes. With some shock I realized that Molly has become hard of hearing.

My first reaction was — Hell! Now I can't rely on the noise to change her mind. She doesn't even hear it, it means *nothing* to her, then I was immediately ashamed of that thought and strangely enough, my anger and impatience faded.

I have decided for the time being, to give up asking Molly to reconsider selling the property. I will leave her in peace. I could weep for the pathetic person she has become. I will not worry her further but try to fall into her way of living and thinking. Try to make her life as pleasant as possible.

For some years now I have been buying the provisions and food that cannot be delivered to the house. I had done it carelessly, with bad grace, but now I am shopping with more thought to food that Molly might fancy. Recently, with some embarrassment, I realized that my wife has not bought herself one new article of clothing for years. I noticed her patched, worn underwear that hung on the laundry line, and I noted that Molly never wore stockings and that her shoes were worn out. For years she had gone every ten days or so to have her hair shampooed and set, but these days her hair is neglected; it grows wispily, and it is almost completely white.

I blamed myself for not having noticed such things before. It was because, I suppose, like her deafness, these things have come about so gradually.

I went shopping and purchased underwear, a pleated skirt, two blouses, shoes. I left the packages on Molly's bed, and later on, I watched as she placed the underwear in a drawer, hung the skirt and blouses carefully on hangers. She had smoothed the material with her garden-rough hands and I was pleased that I had also bought hand lotion, complexion cream, a lipstick, other small feminine necessities, and although Molly appeared to be pleased, she continues to wear her worn clothing, and her hands remain uncared for. The lipstick — never used — stands perched on her dressing table resembling a shiny cartridge.

Young Jodie, now eighteen, has married her Bill. There had been an unpleasant evening when she had come running to our house, crying hysterically, announcing that she was 'going to have a baby' and that she and Bill just 'had to get married' and that they had no chance of getting a decent place to live. She had broken down and wept, pleading with Molly to change her mind and sell our property.

'You and Bill will manage,' Molly had said, quietly. 'It's not good for young people to rely help from their elders. You get married, Jodie, and you'll see, everything will be all right.'

Molly speaks in the strangely hollow voice of a deaf person. I know of course that she is not absolutely deaf. She hears quite well when one speaks directly to her and if there are no conflicting sounds in the nearby vicinity.

Young Rob has gone off to live with Jodie and Bill. Before leaving home he had said to me, 'Uncle John, ever since Jodie left home, Dad has been like a lost soul. Of course, she had always been his special pet, Mum always resented that. I never have. I feel selfish leaving Dad, but it is so damned dreary living with him. Do you think I am being selfish?'

'Not at all,' I had replied and Rob had looked relieved, he had grinned happily, then frowning, he had glanced across the room at Molly, murmuring, 'Uncle John, Aunty Molly is going quite crazy. She could be put away — I mean — she needs treatment of some kind, she has become a bit of a freak.'

I reprimanded him, reminding him of Molly's past kindness to him, to his sister, and he had the grace to look ashamed, and that evening, after Rob left, I asked Molly, carefully, clearly, whether she had heard Rob's remarks. When she said that she had not, I was relieved and I told her that Rob was leaving home, going off to live with Jodie.

'Ralph'll be lonely,' was her only comment, but a few nights later she had awakened me and I sat up in my dark bedroom, startled, for she never came to my room at night.

'What is it?' I asked. 'Molly, are you ill?'

'No,' she replied flatly, 'John, you would never try to have me put away, would you?'

'Ye gods, of course not, Molly! Don't you worry about such things.'

In the same flat voice she told me that she was not at all worried, it was just that she would dislike the trouble and embarrassment that would come about in our peaceful life if I did attempt any such foolish thing.

I spent a sleepless night, worrying about her and about the life we led that she called peaceful. I also wondered whether Molly had been truthful in saying that she had not overheard Rob's harsh remarks. I decided to be more than ever kind and gentle towards her, but also, more watchful in the future.

Soon after his son's departure from home, Ralph went off on a vacation. His firm has given him three months' long service leave, and Ralph told me that he was going to spend his time searching for Ruth in various country towns.

The morning he left his home, I had watched Ralph dodging Molly, who had seemed determined to have words with him. Ralph, just as determinedly, was intent on not letting himself in for a farewell scene.

Whilst Molly stood at the Moystons' back door, knocking and calling, Ralph had hustled from the front door and coming over to me, he had said, 'John, here's an extra front door key. I am renting the house whilst I'm away. Will you give the key to the agent when he calls for it?' He handed the key to me.

I was surprised, but said I would. 'Also, Ralph, you had better leave a forwarding address, just in case,' I said.

'No, no I won't do that, John. I can't really, I have no idea where I'll be. I'll keep in touch. I shall write to you every so often, let you know how I'm doing,' his voice quavered, 'John, I have the strongest intuition! I know — just know — that I'm going to find Ruth.'

'I hope so, Ralph. It's been a long, worrying time for you. You've taken it bravely; I admire you.'

He was pleased with my praise and I asked him — because I felt that it might be true — whether or not he was acting not on intuition alone, but on some information that Ruth actually had been seen by someone in the district he was about to travel to. He replied, saying he would prefer not to tell me more than he already had, for he felt the virtue would go out of his plans if he talked too much about them.

'But,' he repeated, 'I'll keep in touch, John.' Then he had smiled whimsically, saying, 'I have never liked goodbyes. Say goodbye to Molly for me?'

'Yes, of course, and good luck!' I called after him as he walked away. He certainly deserved a holiday, I thought, even if he was going a strange way about it. A vision of Ruth Moyston flashed through my mind. Ruth, so overbearing, so loud mouthed. I wondered about her. Has she also changed very much? As much, say, as poor Molly?

I went over to the Moystons' to tell Molly that it was useless knocking on the door or calling out any more, because Ralph had already departed, and later on, I asked her why she had wanted to speak so urgently to Ralph.

She had replied wearily, saying, 'Urgently? I merely wished to say goodbye to Ralph, and, oh yes, there was a matter I had wanted to discuss with him . . .' After a short pause she continued on, saying, 'He might never come back to his lonely life here.'

Her voice was gentle and wistful. We were standing by the rock-garden and she seemed to be addressing her words to it, rather than to me.

'Ralph! Never come back?' I laughed, 'Why should you think that, Molly? Of course Ralph will come back, he has only got three months' leave.'

'Yes, of course!' she murmured. 'Only three months.'

Molly wandered off to the tool-shed and I returned to the house. It was Sunday. The neighbourhood was quiet and I intended to spend the day cleaning and polishing.

I got to work with the noisy, outmoded vacuum cleaner and I remembered that I had not asked Molly what it was that she had wished to discuss with Ralph. I wasn't especially interested but I decided to ask her later on that evening. However, certain events prevented me from doing so.

During the afternoon, the house agent that Ralph had spoken of came to pick up the key. He was accompanied by another man, a possible tenant, I presumed. His face was vaguely familiar. I looked at him more closely, then I exclaimed, 'Of course! Mr Grey! I remember you! You made those enquiries into the disappearance of our neighbour, Mrs Ruth Moyston! What a coincidence! I mean a coincidence if you rent their house!' And I added, 'She is still missing! Did you know?'

'Yes,' he said with a grin, 'I never lose interest in a case I have been involved in, especially if it remains unsolved.' He told me that if the Moyston house was suitable he would rent it. Then he said thank you, and goodbye, and went off to view the shabby, run-down dwelling.

I went back to my house cleaning and I kept at it until I heard Molly, who was in the bathroom, retching as though she were about to die.

Against her wishes, I called a doctor, who, after examining her, said that the only explanation he had for her condition was extreme nervous tension. He left some sleeping tablets and I was surprised when she more than obeyed his orders and swallowed not one tablet, but two.

CHAPTER FIVE

Ruth, ANOTHER LETTER HAS ARRIVED from the real estate company offering an even higher price for our property. Oh, how lovely — how splendid — it would be if we were able to sell, to move away, leave this hated tract of cultivated garden; to move, live, high up in an apartment, never again to smell soil and grass, the rankness of weeds and the sickly-sweet perfume of flowers. How lovely — how splendid it would be.

Ruth, I hid the letter away along with others that have come before it. There are five in all. I have never let John know about these letters. It would only hurt him all over again. My heart aches for John but I envy him too, because his life — compared to mine — is clear and straightforward. No sword is held to his head. He awakes each day, I suppose, to frustrations and disappointments and dissatisfactions, but I awake to terrors that John could not even imagine.

Ruth, I think that I am losing my reason, because although I am chained here — to you — I feel that I am adrift, that I am floating and I am desolate and frightened of my floating state.

It is useless talking to you like this, Ruth. I know that, I know that it is as useless as describing the pain caused by a bee sting to someone that has never felt a bee sting. I know that it is foolish to do so much of my work here, by the rock-garden, but I get a sense of comfort from being near you, for you alone — now that Ralph has gone — know what I have done and how I have feared and schemed, and only you know how frightened I am of Mr Grey.

I am frightened of dying too, frightened of God. It is my fear of God that prevents me from taking my life. Ruth, before you went, death held no fears at all, apart from the usual fears of the actual pain of it happening. I imagined heaven as a place beneath another sky — higher, bluer — I thought of heaven as a place where John and I would laugh more often, where we would meet with fresh, never before known and happy experiences, and where it would be forever summer. Now, guilts and lies have made me unfit for heaven. When I die I shall be cast out! Cast out into outer darkness! Doesn't that sound fearsome? It is! It *is* fearsome.

Ruth, the day Mr Grey came back here was almost as dreadful as that other day — I mean, the day I dug the hole you lie in. When he arrived, I was here, by you. John was in the house and I saw a man in your garden. For a flash, I had thought it was Ralph come back then I realized that the man was taller, broader and younger than Ralph.

He, the man, walked about, looking the place over. He glanced in my direction, and called to me, saying, 'How are you, Mrs Blake?'

I ignored him and went on pruning the crepe myrtle tree, but he came right up to the dividing fence and I recognized him. I was terribly brave, Ruth, I smiled, pointed to my ears and he seemed to understand what I meant, and he went down the path and rang at our front door.

Something broke — in my mind. I will never be the same again. Damage has been done to my mind. How could it be otherwise? No human being could suffer such an unexpected shock, and recover completely.

I steadied down after a while and although I felt certain that Ralph had contacted Mr Grey and told the truth to him, I was overcome by a great feeling of relief.

I had gone into the house with relief in my heart, because I knew that the end was coming for me. The thing I had dreaded for so long became a welcome thing, and when I heard Mr Grey and John talking together, all I wanted to do was to hurry, to be with John when he heard what Mr Grey had to tell him.

Ruth, it is not all over at all! You are still just missing and Mr Grey says that he has not come here about your disappearance. He has come, so he says, because he has sold his own house and has bought one of the apartments they are building next door and decided that it would be simpler to live nearby until his apartment is completed. He told John that he had asked an estate agent to find him a place, and the agent told him that Ralph was looking for a short-term tenant.

Mr Grey is delighted, so he says, to be near his new home-to-be, and he and John have taken to playing chess together in our living room. John likes him, and if it were any other man in the world but Mr Grey, I would be delighted, for John's sake; but it is Mr Grey, and, Ruth, it is all too much of a coincidence for me to rest easy under. Do you agree? Do you think, as I do, that Mr Grey is here for other reasons?

Ruth, Jodie now has her baby. It is a boy. She brings the little thing here to see John. You remember how he likes children? The baby is called after John, and he is proud of that. Seeing John with the baby brings back my regret in not having been able to give him a child of his own.

He was born to be a father. He is still extremely kind to Jodie and Rob, always ignoring Rob's worsening stutter and patiently advising Jodie about her sudden outbursts of uncalled for hysteria, sympathizing with her because she still bites her finger nails down to the quick. Yes, both your children retain the nervous tics your cruelty induced into them just as they both have certain scars on various parts of their bodies.

Nevertheless, I have to admit that I have taken a dislike to Jodie. She is becoming a thoughtless, an unkind person in many ways. When they all sit together in my living room, petting and admiring the baby, they all, especially Jodie, go on as though I were not in the room, as though I were invisible. On one occasion, they all trooped out to admire this rock-garden, leaving the baby in the living room with me. Then, Jodie had yelled out — just as you used to yell — ordering Bill to return to the house, screaming wildly, 'Hurry, I don't want Johnny left with that mad woman.'

Mad woman! Ruth, you know that all during her childhood, I was the one Jodie came to for comfort and solace and that I never failed her.

As for Rob, poor lad, he is also unthoughtful and unkind towards me. Not so long ago he went so far as to encourage John to have me put away. I gather that he meant I belonged in a lunatic asylum. Yes, they would like that because then, of course, these two fall-down houses could be sold. I don't want to think about that.

I would like to tell those children of yours, Ruth, that if it had not been for your child-bashing tactics, your sadism, I would be a different person indeed from the wreck I have become; and instead of not selling the property, we would have sold it — yes, if we go deeply into the matter, it is your fault alone that things are the way they are, and that *you* are where you are.

Ruth, it is frustrating to me having Jodie speak of you as though you had been the tenderest of mothers to her. 'Oh . . .' she gurgles, 'If only Mum could see you, Johnny. Poor Johnny, your Nana would have loved you so much.'

Ruth, you know as well as I that the only motherly tenderness Jodie knew in her youth came from me. You were too hard, Ruth. I am repeating myself I know, but you were too cruel and it appears to me to be a great injustice that you are now revered and loved by Jodie and Rob, whilst I am despised, scorned and disliked. Yes, you are the blame for so much, so much. It was those years that Ralph spent under your domination that made him into a man who could cover up a crime rather than have the person who had committed it suffer punishment. He was weary of the perpetual chastisement that went on in his home.

Ralph's outrageous behaviour on that dreadful day was the result of the behaviour pattern he had been forced into by your domination, your viciousnesss towards his children. It could not have been otherwise, and you, Ruth, know, even better than I, how Ralph loved Jodie, and Rob, how tender and patient a father he was — and still is. He knew that if he had stood up against you, you would only have made things worse for them.

I know, Ruth, that I have told you on countless occasions how Ralph had said — on that dreadful day — that he admired my courage in facing up to you.

Courage? Oh, dear God, if only I had had even a *modicum* of courage on that day. If only I had not been so cowardly, so filled with conceits about my reputation — such false, such self-important, ridiculous little conceits.

Too late now to think how things could have been, but talking things over helps me. Ruth, when Ralph comes home I will take things a bit easier. He will be pleased because I know I have often upset him on those occasions when I have attempted to talk things over with him. He has been very wise, because never acknowledging to one another what happened has made it seem — not to me — but to Ralph, that nothing actually did happen. If he had made it possible for us to talk, I might have broken down. Yes, I could so easily have broken down and . . .

Ruth, John has had several letters from Ralph and I find hidden messages between the lines. For instance, when he wrote, 'I sincerely hope that my tenant is not a troublesome neighbour in any way' I take that as a message from Ralph to me, warning me to be careful. I am being careful. Dear God, how Ralph would worry and sympathize if he knew that Mr Grey was the tenant.

Oh, Ruth, I am finding it so difficult to be on guard all the time. It is John's fault. When he was annoyed with me, and always unhappy, it was easier, but his recent kindness makes me feel as though I were being beaten, and I have to double my vigilance to prevent myself from breaking down. If I broke down, just think what would happen! No, I will not go into that. It is better not to.

Life is a series of threats and battles. There are always new threats and battles to fight. The latest threat is my tendency to drop off to sleep. I am always dropping off into little dozes, it is nerve-racking, horrible. I was dozing out here one day last week, and I felt the warmth of the sun lessen — that is how light my little naps are — I opened my eyes to see a pair of men's shoes on the grass before me. I looked higher, then higher, and Mr Grey was standing over me. He had not heard the interior scream I had given, but he was aware that he had startled me. He smiled and apologized, saying that he had merely come over to make sure that I was all right. 'I was watching you for some time,' he said, 'There is a cold wind blowing. I felt concerned . . .'

He is an extremely nice man but his eyes appear to see through things, rather than merely to be looking at them, and that day, I had the impression that he was not only looking at this rock-garden but down — beneath it.

When I was able to speak, I had queried his remark and he had repeated the same words but in a louder, clearer voice. In reply, I told him that I rise very early every morning, and that sometimes during the day I take little naps.

'Half your luck,' he said, and then he told me that he admired my work, that he had never seen a more beautiful garden. 'Why,' he asked, 'don't you enter it in a garden contest?'

I told him that I would rather not, and he said, 'That's a pity Mrs Blake, but, unless of course there is something in the garden you want to conceal, you should allow others to share this beauty.'

Ruth, I had broken out into a cold sweat. Can you understand the strain I am living under? I smiled up at him, I kept on smiling as he talked on, saying, 'You devote so much time to this garden — all day and every day — and especially on this magnificent rock-garden.' He had laughed, teasingly, saying, 'Are you *sure* there is no special magic you use to cause its great beauty?'

I had not broken down. I kept on smiling. Mr Grey put his hand on my shoulder, and I did not shudder, as he smiled again, saying, 'I'm sure that no hoard of buried treasure could be lovelier than the flowers you grow.'

He had gone back to his own house and I went inside. I was sick again, retching, as I had retched the day when he first arrived to live here.

Ruth, I have no privacy! Mr Grey and John are becoming as thick as thieves. He, Mr Grey, is in our house nearly every evening, and because the apartment building is nearing completion, I have to bear the burden of being looked over nearly all the time.

Ruth, you know how I used to have those weeps of mine out here, and how sometimes I would cry out loudly, and how I used to feel a little easier after I had let go — I cannot do that any more.

I know that you cannot see me, Ruth, but if you could, you would see that even when I talk to you these days, I never move my lips and this is because I heard two of the men from the building site discussing me. They are a rough gang of men. I have no time for any of them, especially, I dislike the one who called out, 'Hey, take a gander at the old duck, Mac! She's as mad as a meat axe. No, it's OK, she can't hear; she's deaf as a post! Go on — take a look — she's talking away — to herself. Thinks she's got a mate with her. Real old rag-bag, eh?'

He has never heard me speak aloud again.

Restraint! Yes, I am becoming exhausted having to restrain myself so much, and all the time.

That man's expression — rag-bag — gave me a nasty jolt,

and for the past week or so I have been wearing the clothes that John bought for me. John was pleased to see me wearing them, but it made me sad to see him happy for so deluded a reason. I am dressing up for the workmen and especially for Mr Grey — not for John.

But am I making an error? Should I begin to change my ways? I do not know what to do, I am so scared, so…

CHAPTER SIX

SEEING MOLLY wearing her new clothes and with her hair neatly groomed, is the best thing that has happened for some time. My hopes rise about her and about the matter of selling the property.

The real estate company is still interested in purchasing — still want to buy our property. Recently, during one of my house clean-ups, I came upon some letters hidden away beneath the rug in Molly's bedroom. Molly — unknown to herself — has the makings of a good business woman. The purchase price offer has been more than doubled.

A hope is rising in me that perhaps Molly and I do have some chance of a reasonable life ahead, for when I arrived home from work one evening, there was Molly dressed in her new blue blouse, pleated skirt and wearing the palest trace of lipstick. The table was set for dinner. That was more than enough to encourage me, but when I heard Molly's laugh coming from the kitchen, tears actually came to my eyes, and I paused for a moment before calling, as I had not done for years, 'Molly — I'm home!'

She did not answer me, for of course she could not hear, but when I went into the kitchen, she smiled, saying, 'You're home, John!'

'Yes,' I said and kissed her cheek and if Grey had not been in the room I would have broken down just for the wonder of it all.

'Hullo, Blake,' Grey smiled, saying, 'Your wife has taken pity on me and has invited me to dinner.'

I felt let down when Molly did not sit at the table with us, but I realize that if she is recovering, it will be a slow process and I must not expect too much, too soon. It seems as though her hearing is also improving. She still speaks only when spoken to, but it is in a more natural manner, not as though she has a pain getting her words out and if these improvements continue I am going to do my utmost to have the doctor examine her leg, for her limp is as pronounced as ever.

That evening, when dinner was over, Grey and I had a tussle over the chess board; he was the victor as usual. After the match we sat for a while and chatted.

Molly sat by the window, plaiting the bright red raffia that she uses to bind about her potted plants and I must have been looking at her with some tenderness because Grey caught my eye and smiled, saying, 'She's a nice person, that wife of yours. She lives in a dream world of her own, doesn't she?'

'Yes,' I replied, 'and having you as our neighbour is doing a lot for her.'

'Nonsense,' he smiled. 'But I do notice quite a difference both in her appearance and in her manner. If I were you, John, I would take her away for a vacation. Away from the monotony and the routine of . . .'

'I don't think that Molly would agree to that — yet,' I interrupted, and I noticed that Molly had begun plaiting again. Her hands had become motionless during Grey's speech, 'There is a time for everything, isn't there!' I finished off, and Grey gave an understanding nod.

Knowing Grey has made quite a difference in my life too. We have a great deal in common. Until I met up with him again, I had not realized what a well-read man I have become. For the past few years I have read myself ragged. I had begun with light novels, often getting through one in an evening, and sometimes picking up another book and beginning it, but eventually, I had tired of such trivial works, and I had asked the librarian to advise me on my choice of books, and she — glad I suppose to have someone interested — produced wonders for me.

When I return my books to the library, the librarian, Miss Prentice, talks them over, discusses them with me, and she and I have become quite friendly because of our mutual interest and I look forward to my twice-weekly visits to the library and before Grey had arrived in the neighbourhood I had almost made up my mind to take Miss Prentice's advice and join the weekly discussion group held on Friday evenings in the reading room.

She, Miss Prentice, seemed rather disappointed when I told her that I had decided not to join, and for the first time I had mentioned Molly, saying, 'My wife is not very well and so I don't like leaving her by herself in the evenings.'

Miss Prentice, Lorraine, had concentrated on filling in my card. 'That's a pity!' she had said and she appeared flustered, but the next time I saw her she was her usual cool self, and she had handed me a copy of *Shakuntala*, an Indian play, written in the fifth — or as she pedantically said, in or *about* the fifth century — 'You have a real feast in store, John,' she told me, 'This play is a high-water mark in Asian literature.'

Grey had already read *Shakuntala*, and we had some fine evenings together, discussing the work, both arguing and agreeing. I greatly admire the play and instead of returning it, I keep paying dues on it.

One evening when Grey and I were in the midst of a pithy discussion, Jodie had arrived, bringing young John with her. She only comes to visit when she is certain that I will be at home, and as fond as I am of Jodie and the child, I resented her breaking into my talk with Grey.

It had turned out to be a jerky, uncomfortable visit, because Jodie had not then been aware that my guest was her father's tenant, and she stared at Grey crying out with wild excitement. 'But — you are the policeman who was in charge of Mum's disappearance. You are Mr Grey.' Her cute face became puzzled and hopeful, 'Have you news of Mum? Has mum been found? Tell me — *tell* me . . .'

'No,' Grey sounded embarrassed as he kindly explained that Mrs Moyston's whereabouts was still a mystery, saying, 'It must be a great worry to you. Your mother is one of many missing persons.'

'Missing?' Jodie had cried out, 'Mr Grey, I don't think my mother is just *missing*. All Mummy's interests were in her home and in us, her husband, her children. She had *no other* interest in the world and no friends that *I* ever knew of. I believe something awful has happened to Mum.'

She began to cry and I took her hand, attempting to comfort her, but she withdrew it, brusquely, and asked Grey why he had come if it was not about her mother.

'Oh, well, a cop is not on duty all the time,' he said, and he explained to Jodie that he had rented her father's house.

Jodie was surprised, but she quietened down, and during the hour she stayed she commented on Molly's improved appearance.

I was pleased to see that she was kinder to Molly than she had been for some time, even asking, 'Would you like to nurse Johnny, Aunty Molly?'

Looking rather pleased, Molly held out her arms, but the child snuggled against his mother and began howling. We all felt embarrassed, and Molly's face took on the hurt expression one always shows when a child refuses one's advances and certainly Jodie improved nothing by declaring in the obnoxious manner of young mothers, 'There, there, precious, Mummy has got you all safe.'

Fond of Jodie as I am, I was pleased when she left, and also pleased when Grey offered to drive her home. It saved me from having to walk to the bus stop with her, but after they had gone Molly had another violent retching attack and I became annoyed when she flew into a fury, refusing to have the doctor called.

After Molly went off to bed, I took up my copy of *Shakuntala*, and read, ' "I am indeed, deeply in love: but cannot rashly disclose my passion to these young girls . . ." ' I lost myself again in a romance of ancient days.

CHAPTER SEVEN

RUTH, I RESEMBLE A PERSON who has an endless race to run. A race in which the goal recedes as I run. My loneliness is decimating me and sometimes I go to the Bible. I open it at random to try to find comfort and this morning I read from the Book of Job, ' "Fear came upon me, and trembling, which made all my bones to shake." '

No comfort in those words, but closing the book I realized that I had read a description of myself. Fear has been upon me for so long now and I become more and more fearful.

Ruth, ever since that night when Mr Grey drove Jodie and the baby home from our place, he, Mr Grey, has been different. I tell myself that I am only imagining things, but that does not help me at all.

He is not different in his kindly attitude towards me, it is the way he stands at his kitchen window, he just stands there staring out at the garden, and at my garden too, and it is in the way he now inveigles John into talking about our life before he met us, and John talks away to him with a freedom and frankness that makes me want to scream. Yesterday evening John said, 'Yes, Grey, Molly and I were sorry from the very beginning that the Moystons were our neighbours.'

'Sorry?' Mr Grey had broken in on John's spiel, 'But, John, you speak well of Jodie, of her brother and of Moyston.'

'Oh, yes, most definitely,' said John, 'Ruth was the fly in the ointment. It was Ruth's treatment of her children that caused our distress. The woman has a violent temper. She always took sadistic pleasure in scaring, bashing away at them. Not just straight out disciplinary punishments, but she would go to endless trouble to trick the kids into mis-behaviour, and she was openly jealous of Ralph's love for Jodie, and poor little Jodie always got more than her share of chastisements.'

'Quite a she-devil, eh?' said Mr Grey, as John paused and as though John was the best raconteur in the world, and that he, Mr Grey, could not bear for him not to continue.

John did continue, and Ruth, as he spoke on, even I felt that he was exaggerating your cruelty and your ugly cha-racter. John reads too much these days. His mind is over-nourished. When I actually heard him declare that many a time, *I* had gone over and interfered on the children's behalf, also that once, he had actually heard me say that I could kill you for your wickedness. I *had* to stop him, but I could think of no way of doing so. I was amazed at John's vivid imagination in saying that I had gone *many times* to interfere. For of course as *we* both know, Ruth, to our undoing I went but once.

And another thing, Ruth, a new law has been passed. I sat by, apparently calm, listening as John and Mr Grey casually discussed a new law proclaiming that a parent known to be abusing a child must be reported to the auth-orities. This is a bitter pill for me to have to swallow . . .

I had no way of stopping John and when eventually their conversation moved on to other subjects, Mr Grey became rather vague and soon excused himself, saying that he was tired and needed to hit the hay.

He said goodnight to John and he waved goodbye to me, not bothering to speak. He was not being impolite for he believes that it is difficult for me to hear, although these days I allow a little more sound to register. I waved back a goodnight to Mr Grey and after Mr Grey had left, John went off to bed. I said that I would follow soon, but I remained sitting in my chair. I sat there until morning.

I had lost my power to move, to think.

When John discovered me in the morning, he was most upset. He made tea for me and suggested that I spend the day in bed. I said that I would. I told John that I had foolishly fallen off to sleep the night before, and he looked sorry and upset about me. Then he went off to work and I came out here, as you already know.

Time passes very slowly, Ruth. I will be glad when Ralph returns. We are expecting him home shortly. His three months are nearly up.

I overheard Mr Grey telling John that his new apartment would be ready for him to move into just about the time that Ralph returns home, so it appears, Ruth, that I am going to be stuck with Mr Grey for the rest of my life, and my great hope is that my life will not drag on and on.

There is not so much confusion and noise on the building site any more. The work is nearly all interior work now.

Dear God! Ruth! I have just had a frightening, a shocking experience! This morning four strange men entered this garden and walked towards me — right here — to the rock-garden. They surrounded me — all four of them — I just stood here, I did not know what they wanted, but I felt, as I have told you, surrounded.

'Good morning to you!' the tallest one said. 'This garden of yours does you credit. I've never seen anything prettier.'

He had gestured to this rock-garden, saying, 'I certainly hope we won't have to spoil *that*!' and he went on to say that he and his men had come to look over the property, to find out where the sewer and drainage pipes were. They were plumbers and the Council was going to renew the sewer pipes and . . . and . . . And do you know that people *can* fly, Ruth? They *can*. I did, I flew — well perhaps 'fly' is not exactly the word, but certainly I have no recollection of walking. Somehow, I moved from the garden to the living-room. I searched for, and found, the plans of our land, and in a floating-like trance I returned to the garden and handed them to the boss-man, and it seemed as though a swarm of bees buzzed about my head, and I swear that my feet did not touch the ground. They seemed to remain a few inches above it, and then, one of the men said, 'Good news for you! All the piping is in the front of your property, so we won't have to muck up your nice garden after all!' My feet thumped down, hitting the ground so hard that my head jerked back sharply, and I had to move my arms wildly, to brush the bees away.

'Are you all right?' one of the men asked, and I nodded my head, then the men all walked away, towards the front of the house, but suddenly, one of them stopped short, and came back — here — to the rock-garden. The other men waited and watched him, and I watched him too as he closed his eyes and began sniffing at the air, and Ruth, it is a difficult subject to bring up, especially to you, but when that man began sniffing, I began sniffing too, and there was a *shocking* stench. The other men joined us, and all five of us stood sniffing and looking at each other, questioningly, then I remembered — it was the blood and bone fertilizer. I leapt over to the sack-covered heap of fertilizer and really I felt like a stage magician as I lifted the sacking up, holding it away from my side, the way a toreador holds his scarlet cloth when he has foiled the bull. I laughed, loudly, and the men laughed too, and they laughed all the way down the side path to the front of the house.

Ruth, I am still standing here. Standing exactly where they left me. I am still holding the sacking in my hands. I feel strange. I feel so strange. I am unable to move . . .

CHAPTER EIGHT

I AM DEEPLY CONCERNED. I do not know what is going to become of Molly. Returning home from work, I found her lying in the garden, lying on an old piece of sacking. She was unconscious.

The doctor examined her thoroughly, and after the examination he spoke to me seriously, saying that he was quite puzzled, and was insistent, saying, 'Mr Blake, your wife is definitely under some great strain. Are you sure that you have told me all you can about her?'

'Yes,' I had replied, 'Yes, I am certain. Quite sure! Until the question came up about selling this house and moving away, my wife was an ordinary contented woman.'

'But you have told me before that you have let the matter of selling your property go by the board, so to speak. Is Mrs Blake still nervous about that? Even if she were . . .' he continued, thoughtfully, 'I don't believe that it would cause such tensions in her. There has to be something else. Now, I want her to remain in bed for a few days, at least, and I want you to be certain to have the sedative I am prescribing put in her milk drinks. I especially do not want Mrs Blake to know that she is having a sedative.' He smiled, saying, 'She is a nice patient, but very stubborn. You know, Mr Blake, she reminds me of a bird, you know how birds move their heads from side to side, always on the look out for — well — birds, of course, are on the look out for an enemy attack. What is Mrs Blake on the defensive for? *That* is what I would like to know.'

'I wish that I could help more,' I told him. 'By the way,

Doctor, can anything be done about that leg of hers?'

'Leg? Which leg?'

'Her left leg. She has been dragging it for years.'

'I have found nothing wrong with either of her legs. Tell me, did that condition also begin when the property problem arose? It might have begun as a kind of protest, and she has carried the habit on . . .'

The doctor's voice trailed off as Grey walked into the living room. 'Sorry, John,' Grey apologized, 'I'll come back later on.'

'No, don't go, Grey!' I said and I introduced him to the doctor and then I told him that we were discussing Molly's health, explaining that she had experienced rather a nasty turn.

Then speaking to the doctor, I said, 'No. My wife's leg began troubling her some time before that property upset. She had wrenched her ankle, it was a very severe sprain —'

'That's correct!' Grey exclaimed. 'I was here a few evenings after Mrs Blake had sprained her ankle. You remember, John, it was the first time we met!'

'That's right!' I agreed. 'Thinking back, I suppose that was when the change really began in Molly, but apart from the concern that one would normally feel when a neighbour disappears into thin air, neither Molly nor I have given much thought to the matter.'

'I don't recall hearing anything about that case,' interrupted the doctor impatiently. 'Nevertheless, Mr Blake, it could be that the disappearance of her friend has preyed deeply on your wife's mind. I suggest that she have psychiatric treatment.'

'Anything,' I agreed, 'Anything that will help her.'

Before leaving, the doctor said that he would call again in a few days' time and he reminded me to be sure that Molly had her milk drinks and the sedatives.

Grey stayed on for a while but we were both in silent

moods, and when I remarked that it was time for Molly's sedative and milk, he said, 'I'll be off.' Then he hesitated for a moment as though making up his mind to tell me something, but evidently thinking better of it, he said, 'I'll be on my way. Give my best to your wife, John.'

CHAPTER NINE

Having to stay in bed has been a strain but at least I have been able to sleep. Sleep is such a blessing. For years I have spent restless, wakeful nights and now that insomnia has — in the most miraculous way — left me, I feel relaxed and I could lie here for ever if that were possible, but it is not possible and I must fight against this feeling of lassitude, not only of my body but of my mind.

Jodie came to visit with me this morning. I should think John must have asked her to call, because I know she dislikes me. She brought some grapes and she brought flowers. Flowers — to me . . .

Glass has now been placed in the huge windows of the apartment building. The windows glare down at me, and soon, curious eyes will look from those windows. Children will come to live in the apartments. They will have bats and balls and the balls will come over the fence into my garden and I will have less privacy than ever. I shall become surrounded and by people I will never know. People who will never know me. It is lonely, terrible to live in the world without one person you can be open and frank with.

There has been Ruth! I have been frank with her — but from today — I will never talk to Ruth again. This morning, I had begun telling her about Jodie coming over, about the baby and about how weak I have been.

'Ruth,' I had begun.

I had been talking to myself, just standing in my garden, looking at the ground — talking to myself, just as all these years I have known that, but I have kept on, making believe that Ruth could hear me.

I wish that Ralph would hurry home. I am impatient for his return because I am going to talk to him and I do not know how he will take what I have to say. But no matter what he feels, I am going to confess, give myself up! Confess everything! Confess that I accidentally killed Ruth Moyston.

I will not bother about the garden any more. The garden may go to rack and ruin. From force of habit, as I stood there this morning, I plucked a delicate green weed from the rock-garden, and I whispered, tentatively, 'Ruth . . .? Ruth . . .?'

Then, I ceased calling to her. I stood there, thinking to myself, instead of talking to a corpse — I have made a decision, I thought, and the decision has killed the cowardly panic in me. Soon — very soon — I will be free to do the thing I long to do. To confess!

Yes, I am going to confess that Ruth is not missing. That she has been in this secret grave for almost four long years and after the confession I will be free. Free to pray, and after I have prayed, maybe death will become my friend in place of the monster I have dreaded for so long.

I want to act now, today, but I must wait for Ralph to come home. He and I must talk together. He must not be implicated. There is no need for Ralph to be implicated. Although he was wrong — in every way — first, because he believed he had been protecting Jodie; then his protection of me. He was wrong even though he acted from the gentleness of his heart.

His three months' vacation will soon be over and when he returns I will tell him what I am going to do, and we can make plans to keep him completely out of the affair.

I am now glad that Mr Grey lives close by. It will save me the trouble, the embarrassment of having to go to the police. I shall go direct to Mr Grey and Mr Grey might well be embarrassed himself, when he learns that the woman the police have been searching for lies in this very garden, and that Mr Grey has, many times stood both on and beside her grave. He will be shocked. Many people will be shocked, and I — who have lived through so many shocks — I am sorry for them all.

I cannot fully understand why this wondrous calm has come so suddenly to my storm-tossed mind. I am less distracted. Even my thoughts have become precise. I am able to sleep at night. Every night — since I have been ill — ever since that evening when John came home and found me lying unconscious in the garden, I have fallen into deep and restful sleep. Perhaps it is a sign that my inner suffering, that my terrible punishment, is coming to an end and that God is showing His grace to me.

When I come out with the awful truth, I hope that Mr Grey will understand I am confessing because I want to — of my own accord — and not because I am suspicious of his suspicions. He has his suspicions, I am convinced of that. I am certain that Mr Grey suspects that Ruth should no longer be just a name on the Missing Persons list.

It is imperative that I speak to Ralph before I speak to Mr Grey. It is desperately important, for if Ralph is caught unaware he could give away more than is necessary and that could do him irreparable harm.

Yes. Yes, the glass has been fixed into the windows of the new apartment building. People — men, women and children — will soon move in and make their homes there.

I am glad that this ugly business will be over before the people arrive. It would not be a good omen for the new tenants' future happiness if they looked from their windows, down upon the garden, to see, to witness . . .

I will not think of what is going to happen. I shall wait quietly for Ralph to return, and for today — because I do not think that he will return today — I will not even think any more, but return to my bed and maybe fall into one of those little dozes that I used to be so scared of.

I had been unable to doze off because of the noise in the

street. The Council men are going full steam ahead laying the new sewerage and drain pipes in our front garden and right along the street.

They make a great deal of noise — the noise is unendurable — and I can no longer control the volume of sound I hear. I wonder if my hearing is actually beginning to play up, in fact, after the years of pretence? Not with a loss of hearing but hearing too loudly.

It would be so comforting, so wonderful, to have someone to talk to, someone who could perhaps feel even a modicum of pity for me, for my plight.

Today, I saw — as though for the first time — the garden I have created, the garden I have hated and have slaved over, and I recognized its beauty. The garden is beautiful.

I noticed the camellia bushes, so gleaming, so green! Soon, small buds will show, hard and tight with the promise of blossoms to come. I shall leave those buds to blossom as they will. I wonder if John will notice the camellia flowers? He has changed so much. He looks so healthy, so handsome. I love him so much, so deeply.

In comparison to John, I am so elderly, so weary and so lonely. What has happened to my life? Where has it gone? What has happened to John and me?

I know that I am foolish to pretend that I do not know why things are as they are. I know that, but this morning, when I saw my white hair in the mirror, saw and realized how lined and how sharp my face has become, it almost broke my heart, but all that does not really matter, because as though a miracle has occurred, my mind has become like a still pool in the centre of a whirlpool. I have not only stopped running, my direction has changed. I know where I am going. I have confidence. My goal will not recede as I walk, I hope, unlimpingly towards it.

CHAPTER TEN

THE LAYING of the new sewerage pipes is making our street hazardous and chaotic. When the Council men knock off from work every day, they leave red-light lanterns to warn of the path's pitfalls.

Yesterday evening returning home from work, just as I was about to enter my gate, Grey beckoned to me from the Moystons' front door, calling, 'John, spare me a moment, or two?'

'What's on your mind?' I asked and he told me that he was almost certain he had seen Ralph Moyston in the city. 'Ralph?' I had exclaimed. 'So he's back in town! Well, actually he is only a few days earlier than expected.'

Grey said, 'John, if it were Moyston I saw, he has been back for some time, probably has never been away.'

I laughed that suggestion off, saying that I was sure he was mistaken, but Grey went on to say that he, and a colleague of his, had been in one of the dockside pubs, the old Castle Hill. He explained, 'You know what a dump that pub is.'

'No,' I said, 'I don't know. Pubs have never played much of a part in my life.' I was not impressed with Grey's story because I know that Ralph — like myself — never frequents hotels of any description, let alone second-rate pubs. 'Grey,' I said, 'Even if it were Ralph that you saw, is there any reason why he shouldn't have been in the Castle Hill pub? I mean, you were there too.' I added.

He grinned, saying, 'Yes, but I'm a bit of a boozer!' and he continued on, speaking seriously, saying, 'John, I was there on a job. I noticed this fellow standing at the bar and I at once thought it was Moyston. I caught the fellow's eye and raised my hand in recognition, but I received a blank — absolutely blank — look in return. The man left the pub and I went to the bar and asked the barmaid, Maisie, if she knew him. Maisie is an old pal of mine and I know that I can rely on her word, she told me that the man in question was a Mr Gorman, a nice chap, who came in every evening for a drink or two, and Maisie had laughed, saying, "Now, Mr Grey, don't tell me *that* nice gentleman has been up to any mischief?"

'For a moment, I accepted the fact that I had been mistaken, then, John, I felt that I had not. "Maisie," I said, "Has he ever shown you a photograph of his wife? Does Gorman ever mention his wife?"

' "He hasn't got a wife," she said. Maisie was becoming impatient and she continued on looking over her shoulder at me, saying, "I know that for a fact, Mr Grey. I also know that Mr Gorman is thinking of getting married — to a real nice lady at that. She comes in here with him quite often. They're real fond of each other. It's very nice to see!" she finished up, primly. You see, John, Maisie is a stickler for the proprieties, she likes to see people happy — and married. Still, I was not satisfied. I asked her where Gorman worked, and she said, "Somewhere about! I think he drives an elevator, in one of the warehouses. Look, Mr Grey, I'm sorry, but this is my busy time." '

Grey had gone on to say, 'It was also my busy time, and so I put Moyston out of my thoughts, but . . .'

'But what?' I prodded. 'Grey, as sure as I am not Napoleon Bonaparte, that Gorman chap is not Ralph Moyston. I know Ralph almost as well as I know myself, and just the thought of Ralph frequenting a low pub, and having a "lady friend" tells me that you are mistaken. Also,' I reminded Grey, 'I have had several letters from Ralph — all from up north-country way.'

I stood up, saying that I had neglected to pick up Molly's

sedative mixture and that if I were to get it before closing time I would have to hurry. The doctor had been firm about not neglecting the sedative and I had given her the last dose in the bottle.

'OK, but hold it, John,' Grey's voice was serious and he looked a bit embarrassed too, 'There is something else I must tell you.'

'Well — go ahead!' I encouraged, and as I listened to what Grey had to say I began to feel extremely uneasy and later on that night, lying in bed, I thought over everything that he, Grey, had told me.

He had begun by saying, 'John, it was pure coincidence when I rented Moyston's house. I had accepted the idea that Ruth Moyston had sickened of housework, of family life, and taken off into the nowhere. It's not unusual, many women do it, and searching for them is like looking for needles in haystacks. They usually turn up sooner or later. I was quite pleased to be so near my new apartment, and by the way — I'll be moving in, very soon now.'

'That'll be nice,' I said, impatiently, wanting to be on my way. 'Very nice!'

'Yes, very nice!' he agreed, then he said, 'I am reluctant to tell you this, but I believe Ruth Moyston's daughter was correct in surmising that her mother is dead, and furthermore, I believe that Moyston was — '

I broke into his spiel, 'You're out of your mind, Grey. That is, if you are implying that Moyston — that Ralph was involved in foul play. In . . .?'

'Hold it! Quieten down! I'm sorry, John, maybe I am being too abrupt.'

I began to breathe evenly again, as he continued on, saying, 'Let me start afresh where I should have begun — with something factual. John, the first time my suspicions were aroused was on the night I drove young Jodie home from your house. She is a great chatterbox, as you know, and that night she talked her pretty head off. I pay little

85

attention to the pleasing picture she gives of her mother. It's only natural that she now sees her mother as a kindly, delightful person. Very few people speak ill of the dead — the missing either, in most cases. Well, that evening, I asked Jodie to go back over the day of her mother's disappearance, see if she had overlooked anything — even the smallest detail — I had encouraged her, not because I was actually interested, but because my mind was on quite another matter and her rapid-fire empty talk was annoying me. I knew that if I got her on to the subject of her mother I need only nod and occasionally say, "Yes, yes, go on . . ." '

'Well, I had been correct and once off she rattled away like a machine gun. I paid little or no attention to the well-worn story — that was, until I heard mention of a spending spree that Moyston had taken her — Jodie — on.

' "What was that you were saying, Jodie?" I asked. "Sorry, I was concentrating on my driving! What was that about a shopping spree?"

' "Oh — that!" She continued on telling me that about a month after her mother had taken off into the blue, her father — Moyston — said it was time she had some nice clothes to wear.

' "Mummy . . ." Jodie cut into her story, " . . .Mummy is a darling but she was awfully strict in some ways. Like, she wouldn't let me use lipstick and she made all my dresses herself and not very well at that! Well, Mr Grey, anyway, Daddy took me shopping. It was wonderful and good fun but I was a bit surprised about the expensive things he let me choose, and a bit worried too, about how when Mummy came home she might blame *me*. But I didn't say anything because Daddy and I were so happy that day, and we got some nice things for Rob too, and it's a bit queer but I never thought about that money till a few days ago . . ." '

Grey had broken off to light a cigarette, then he took up his story again, saying that he had asked Jodie to continue, and she had done so in a puzzled voice, saying, ' "Mr Grey, that day we went shopping, Daddy had a pocket stuffed full of money. Not like the money he always kept in his wallet, but rolled into tight bundles the way my mother kept money in *her* wallet. It's a long time ago, but I'm sure I never thought it queer then — but, about three months ago, just before Daddy went off on his vacation, he left the suit he had worn that day because it was old and shabby and he had never worn it again after our shopping spree. He told me to give the suit away, along with some other old junk.

"Well, I forgot to do as he had asked, but a few days back I remembered, and before I packed the suit and things into a carton, I went through the pockets of the suit and I found an old red plastic wallet. It was Mum's wallet, and it was empty. I felt — well — I felt a bit queer — you know — seeing something of Mum's. I'm sure Dad will be able to explain everything. Really, Mr Grey, that was what made me blow off steam tonight at Uncle John's. I just couldn't believe that Mum would go off leaving the money she had gone to such trouble and through so many fights with Dad, to save."

Grey had gone on, saying, 'Then John, Jodie threw me one of those cute smiles, saying, "Mr Grey, I don't really think Mum is dead. I was just upset, you know — the baby so new and all — and seeing the wallet." '

Grey had talked on, telling me that after he dropped Jodie off he had driven away with his mind buzzing and perturbed.

My own mind buzzed and I also was perturbed, so perturbed that I forgot to pick up Molly's all-important medication, and during the night — a night during which I lay awake tossing and restless — I was aware that Molly also lay sleepless, I heard her tossing and turning and I knew that I should at least offer to take warm milk to her, but my thoughts upset and disturbed me. I began to fanta-size — most atrociously — about the possibility of Ralph having killed his wife. Try as I would I could not get off to sleep, and in the morning I got up, showered, dressed and left the house much earlier than was my wont and without even bothering to take Molly a cup of tea.

This evening, before coming home, I dropped into the library, at first not really understanding why. Not to pick up a new book, but perhaps to delay my homecoming, or just for the utter quiet of the place. Then, I saw Lorraine and I knew why I had gone to the library.

I knew that I was in love with her. Deeply in love!

It was as though a dam had burst in my mind and my heart. I knew that I had never known the meaning of love. I was shattered and just as I was about to move away, Lorraine had glanced up, our eyes met and I knew that I not only loved but that I was loved.

'Lorraine . . .' I moved to her side and as I was about to take her hand in mine, I remembered Molly. I hesitated. I heard Lorraine gasp, softly, in puzzlement and I walked away.

My eyes were blurred and my chest and my throat ached as never before in all the years of my life. I knew that I would never call at the library again. I would parcel up the *Shakuntala*, mail it back to the library.

Life stretched ahead, dismally, and as I reached the familiar corner of our street the problem of Ruth Moyston hit at me with a foreboding force. I had completely forgotten about Ralph too. Lost in the welter of my own emotions, I wanted nothing more than to be alone, to lick my wounds in private.

CHAPTER ELEVEN

LAST NIGHT, insomnia returned to be my sadistic bed-partner, and John had already left the house this morning when I struggled wearily from bed and limped to his room. He had never left for work so early, and never without saying goodbye to me.

I sat on the edge of his neatly made bed. I had wanted to ask him to buy some sleeping pills for me. I knew that I must have them. Never again would I endure another sleepless night. During the long night, I had relived every minute of the past four years, not only once but again and again, I relived it all.

Jodie's anguished weeping... Ruth's figure, turning to face me, the wild, twisted hatred on her face... the menace of her raised arm. The dull thud of her head on the tiled floor. The blood...

The shock of Ralph returning home, of seeing Ralph standing at Ruth's bedroom door.

On and on, and I knew that I must have sedatives. I *must* sleep to be able to face that which lies ahead of me. I would beg the doctor, if necessary. If he were an intelligent, clever doctor, he would have prescribed a sedative for me.

I felt an irreparable sorrow that God's grace was not, after all, being shown to me, and I began to fear death again.

I dressed myself. I made tea and carried it into John's small bedroom. I felt a desperate need for comfort, and in the room where his pipes, his books, his clothes were, I did receive some comfort, and my heart was filled with love for John, for his dearness and his goodness, and I lay on his bed and wept. I wept so much that his pillow became damp. I turned it over and the other side of the pillow also became wet with my tears. I wept because I knew that if I had confided in John from the start, somehow, he would have taken charge. I would have had him behind and beside me, all the way.

After a time, my weeping ceased and I lay dry-eyed. The hours dragged by wearily and the sounds of the neighbourhood seemed to come from another world, and had no meaning to me and instead of the precise, cool, forward-looking mind that I had begun to see as my strength, my mind blurred and dipped and sprang from thought to thought and from memory to memory, and my head began to ache so badly that at times small mewing sounds of anguish escaped from my lips. I despised my weakness but I could not stop those sounds; they were as much beyond my control as an attack of the hiccoughs.

The men on the building site knocked off work and the neighbourhood became deadly quiet. My mewing sounds ceased and I crept from John's room into my own bedroom. I caught sight of myself in the mirror, old and ugly. So old and ugly . . .

I showered, I dressed myself carefully. I brushed my hair for a long time and pinned it neatly. I wanted to look as nice as was possible for John so I used the bright red lipstick he had bought me and I rubbed a little of it on to either cheek. Then once more I examined myself in the mirror and a garish old clown gazed back. I turned away in disgust and with great shame, for I heard John's footsteps approaching the front door.

He had come home a little later than usual. I did not want him to see my ghastly painted face. His footsteps came slowly up the path; they were much slower than usual and I was glad, because it gave me time to wipe the lipstick from my cheeks and lips. I did, but the lipstick smudged and looked worse than ever; then — before I could set it right —

John was already in the house and we encountered each other, face to face, in the hallway.

'Hello, Molly,' he said, flatly, and he went into his room and shut the door.

I knew that he shut the door because he could not bear the sight of me — the old clown — and as I crept along the hallway, covering my smudged, reddened mouth with both of my calloused hands, those little mewing sounds began again.

I went out into the garden — and like an arrow to its target — straight to the rock-garden, where I stood, staring down at the medley of colour, at the flowers and the leaves, the delicate ferns, and my eyes pierced through them, to the soil beneath and further, further down . . .

I covered my eyes but that did not hide what I saw. Not Ruth, not Ruth Moyston's decomposed body, but myself — lying there, staring up.

If only John had not been at home. It was not fair to him, and more — much more — it was not fair to me that my husband should have heard the long, dreadful cat-like yowl that the mewing sounds developed into and knowing that John must have heard, I flung my arms towards the evening sky and I yowled again, in shame and agony, then I saw John come running from the house towards me . . .

CHAPTER TWELVE

THE FOUR WEEKS that went by after Molly's breakdown dragged wearily. Seeming more like three months than one. I felt that I could not do enough to care for my wife, to try and make up for the unfeeling way I had treated her that evening.

On hearing those frightful animal-like howls coming from the rock-garden I stood as though frozen in my bedroom. What was *making* that sound? There was no human element in the weird call, then, at the second spine-chilling howl I ran from the house. Grey arrived at the rock-garden simultaneously with me. It was Grey who gathered Molly into his arms and carried her to the bedroom. I walked beside him, fearful and pitying, as I listened to my wife's stumbling, pathetic little tale of how she had 'tried so hard to look nice for John . . .'

' . . .Brushed and brushed and brushed my hair and brushed . . . the lipstick was too bright . . . made me such a clown . . . so ugly . . . ugly . . .

'John, poor John. I am so ugly, so . . .'

Grey placed Molly on her unmade bed and held her work-worn hands in his. His voice was as gentle as his manner as he told Molly that she was one of the nicest women he had ever known. 'One of the nicest!' he repeated firmly and as he threw a dagger-like look at me, I attempted to take Molly's hands in mine but she hid them beneath her armpits, whispering sanely, and so quietly that we could scarcely hear her, 'Please! Please — may I be alone?'

Grey nodded and tucked the blanket about her and

taking my arm he steered me from the room. 'Poor woman,' he said. 'Poor little thing.' He advised me to call the doctor, at once.

When the doctor arrived he gave Molly an injection, to make her sleep, and then he rounded on me, accusing me of going against his orders by neglecting to give Molly the sedative he had prescribed. I apologized, saying that I had not realized how ill my wife was. Then I suggested that maybe Molly should be in a hospital for treatment.

The doctor replied, saying that he wanted no new pressures, no new upsets for his patient, and that for the time being she must relax, stay in bed but he most definitely wanted a nurse installed in the house, and he had advised, saying, 'I want Mrs Blake to know that she is now receiving sedation.'

I was relieved when the nurse finally left. For one month she ruled the roost and complained about the lack of modern appliances in the home, declaring waspishly, 'No wonder poor little Mrs Blake has broken down. Nothing works in this house, even your vacuum cleaner doesn't work. Mr Blake, aren't you aware of the help other women have in their homes?'

She had gone on and on, day after day, and I had put up with her for Molly's sake. The day she left Molly sat in the living room. She refused to allow me to turn her chair to face the window.

'But,' I suggested gently, 'You could see your garden. You love the garden.'

'No. Please, no, John,' she whispered.

Molly has become a wisp of a woman, her eyes are melancholy and it actually hurts me to look at her, and I feel that she prefers to be alone, so I went off to see Grey who is now installed in his new home.

Before entering the now completed apartment building, looking at the shabbiness of my own home, at the desolated emptiness of the Moystons' house, I was unable to prevent a degree of spleen rising up in me against Molly. Then — what the hell — I thought, and then I faced the fact that my spleen had nothing to do with property. The truth was that I was painfully and deeply in love and unable to do a thing about it.

Grey is inordinately proud of his new home and I complimented him on his excellent taste. Although we are good friends I had never asked about his private life and when, rather abruptly, I asked, 'Grey, have you ever thought about getting married?' he grinned, saying, 'Tried it once, John! Didn't like it!'

Actually, I had gone over to see him hoping for a game of chess, but when I suggested that we get the chess men out Grey had hesitated, then said that he was waiting on an important telephone call, which I took to mean that it was time to make myself scarce; also, I realized, it could be unwise to leave Molly alone for too long a period.

Once back home, I could not settle down and my restlessness made Molly nervous. Every time our eyes met we looked away from one another, almost furtively, and when we spoke it was as though we were strangers.

'Would you like another coffee, Molly?'

'No. No, thank you, John.'

'John, why don't you read?'

'Read? Oh, I have nothing to read.'

I repeated that I had nothing to read and Molly asked me if I had given up going to the library. If there was one place in the world I did not want to be reminded of it was the library. 'No,' I said, 'I just haven't been there lately.'

After a slight pause, Molly said, 'Is Miss Prentice on holidays, John?'

'Who?' I stammered, 'What did you say?'

'I asked you whether Miss Prentice — the librarian — was away on vacation?'

I replied, saying that I had no idea and it took me a

moment or two to realize that Molly could often have heard Lorraine's name mentioned during my talks with Grey.

In a way, I envy Molly. I am desperately sorry that she has become such a mixed-up, neurotic woman, but at least her mind is not in the torment that my mind is in.

I feel quite unable to cope with being in love. No matter how I try, and God knows I try all the time, I find it impossible not to think of Lorraine. I tell myself that I am a conceited, deluded fool, then I recall the way Lorraine looked at me and I know that in no way was I deluded. I knew that she, also, was in love. My longing to see, just to see her, made me edgy, impatient with Molly, which led me into feeling even more edgy.

One afternoon, thinking of Lorraine, I had sighed deeply and looking at Molly, I suggested that maybe she would like to lie down, 'You have been sitting up for hours,' I said, 'Let me help you to your room, make you some coffee and . . .'

As though I had not spoken, Molly spoke, saying, 'John, where is Ralph? He should have been home weeks ago. You must have heard from him? What are you hiding from me? Why hasn't Jodie been to see me? What has been happening during my — my illness?'

Her voice trailed off into silence. I knew that she could not bear to remember that evening by the rock-garden. 'Please, Molly,' I pleaded, anxiously, 'Please don't become so upset, so excited.'

I had reason to be anxious because Molly was standing, clinging to the chair and the red spots on her chalk white face were as vivid as the lipstick spots she had worn a month ago.

'Please, Molly!' I begged and my voice grew louder, for Molly obviously was not hearing me. She had also raised her voice and was rambling on about Ralph, about me, keeping secrets from her and as she continued on, Grey walked into the living room unannounced. He stood watching and listening with interest and also with pity, and whilst Molly continued her incoherent questions, Grey caught my eye, signalling that he wished to speak with me urgently. Then he explained placatingly, to Molly, that Jodie and her husband had been away on a fishing trip.

'They will be returning to the city in a few days' time,' he said, 'And then, of course, Jodie will be over to see you.'

He inveigled Molly into agreeing that she should lie down for a while and when she agreed, he praised her good sense, and he went on to tell her that Ralph Moyston had returned to the city, but that for the time being he had decided not to come back to his old home, preferring to live in a rooming house.

'Now that you are feeling so much better, Mrs Blake,' Grey said gently, 'I am sure that you will be having visitors.'

Molly looked from Grey to me, and back again to Grey. 'Are you speaking the truth?' she then asked quietly.

Grey replied, saying, 'Why should I lie to you? Is something on your mind? If so, would you care to tell me, to confide in me?'

Molly's hands went to her ears as though she were in pain, 'I must lie down,' she said, 'I must lie down . . .'

I helped her to the bedroom, and feeling a rush of tenderness, as I tucked her in, I brushed her forehead with my lips, and her eyes filled with tears, then she turned her face to the wall. I left the room, hurriedly, my own eyes ablur. Strangely, nostalgically, I thought back to that evening, many years ago, when we had been so young and had worn borrowed plumes to go to the theatre.

It seemed a very long time ago. My memories were interrupted by Grey, asking if Molly was all right, and I liked him for his liking of Molly.

'She seems OK,' I replied, 'Poor darling!' Then I smiled, wryly, for I, in all our married life, had never used the endearment 'darling' to Molly. Dear, I had always called her 'dear'.

'John,' Grey interrupted my thoughts again, saying, 'Come out into the yard. I don't want your wife over-hearing what I have to say.'

Standing by the rock-garden, Grey told me that Ralph Moyston was in for trouble, that he had been called in for further questioning about the disappearance of his wife, Ruth Moyston. Grey went on explaining to me that I had been correct in saying that Ralph had left the city to roam around the country districts but that he had not gone alone, that a woman had accompanied him on his travels.

'Yes,' Grey grinned, 'The nice lady, Maisie, my barmaid pal mentioned to me.'

'Just a moment,' I complained. 'Why the hell shouldn't Ralph have a girlfriend and travel with her?'

'No reason why not,' said Grey. 'However, they were away for merely a week or two then on returning to the city they have been living together at the Railway Hotel —'

Again I interrupted, 'Living together! Is that a crime?'

'Cool it, John! Hold your horses!' Grey was becoming impatient. 'Moyston, the fool, had recently applied for a marriage licence — and under his real name at that. I, or I should say, the police who had been watching and waiting, pounced on him.'

I stood aghast and silent. 'It's amazing,' Grey added, smugly, 'What criminals think they can get away with, especially murderers — killers.'

'I can't think of Ralph as a murderer,' I said dazedly. 'If he killed Ruth, it must have been an accident.'

The enormity of the entire thing suddenly struck me. 'Grey,' I said, 'this could be a ghastly business.'

'Yes, it could,' Grey agreed, 'and John, I guarantee you that it will be. Murder is never a pleasant business and I swear a murder took place.' He went on to say that Ralph was running true to form and refusing to answer any questions and that the only statememt he had made was, 'If it is true that my wife is dead, I did not kill her.'

'Maybe . . .?' I began hopefully.

'No, John,' Grey stopped me, 'Moyston is as guilty as hell. Our big problem is that we can't hold him. However, he can't leave the city and will have to report in every day and . . .'

Grey had gone on explaining the intricate machinations of the law to me and then seeing that I was really upset by his news about Ralph, he changed his tone and advised me to keep the news from Molly, saying, 'She will know soon enough, and in my opinion, the later the better. She's in no fit state to deal with this, and of course, you realize that more than likely both of you could be drawn into this sordid business.'

He lowered his voice. 'John, your wife is in for one hell of a shock! If this mess turns out as I think it will, I really do advise you to up stakes, leave this district. I'm no doctor, but I'm certain it would be better for Mrs Blake. New surroundings can work wonders with people's health.' He looked at me hopefully.

I nodded. 'You may be right,' I said. 'You may be right!' And for one giddying second I envisioned the face of Lorraine Prentice.

I closed my eyes on that dream and when I opened them again I saw only the reality of life, the grim years ahead. Grey asked me if I would accompany him while he told Jodie and Rob Moyston about their father.

'No!' I objected, 'Don't ask that of me. I have known them since they were small children. I am deeply fond of them.'

Grey was understanding and went off by himself to do the unpleasant job. I went back inside and prepared tea and toast for Molly, but I ate the snack myself, for she was asleep. The toast tasted like cottonwool in my mouth and the tea was bitter.

Molly stayed in bed all day yesterday and I just loafed around the house, unable to concentrate, not even the Sunday papers interested me, that is, after I had ratted through them with some vulgar curiosity, to see if there was any mention of Ralph. There was no mention.

At a loss, I wandered about the house. I knew that I should go to Jodie and Rob. I knew that they would both be extremely worried about their father, and I knew that Grey would have forbidden them to come to our place. They had probably been instructed not to telephone me either, just in case Molly happened to answer the telephone.

At last, in desperation I went over to Grey's apartment but he was not at home. I was annoyed with him for keeping me in suspense. The least he could have done was to let me know how Rob and Jodie had taken the news.

It was evening when the telephone finally rang and when I heard Grey's voice I was as relieved as a boy is when his girl calls after a lovers' quarrel. 'Where the hell are you?' I yelled. He replied telling me that he was not deaf. That he had spoken to Ralph and that Ralph was still sticking to his statement, that he knew nothing about the whereabouts of Ruth Moyston, either dead or alive.

I was about to ask Grey about Jodie and Rob but hearing a slight sound, I turned and saw Molly clinging to the door frame. 'What is it?' she whispered. 'What is wrong?'

I spoke into the telephone, saying calmly, 'Nothing is wrong, Molly, Mr Grey just wants to know if you are feeling better, and if so would I be free to go and . . .'

'And — what?' Molly asked in the strangest little voice, 'Go and do . . . what . . .?'

'And — what?' came Grey's voice. 'John, do you have to be such a fool? I'm in the city, I am at Headquarters.'

'Oh!' I spoke artificially, 'I was just telling Molly you

wanted me to come over and finish that game of chess.'

'John,' Grey said, with his ability to pick up situations, 'I'll be in touch with you, OK?'

'OK,' I replied and placing the receiver down, I smiled and explained to Molly that Grey sent her his regards and that he wanted to come on the following evening for a game of chess. Then I helped her along the hall, past that room we had once hopefully called the nursery and settling her into bed, I prepared a bowl of soup and sat by her, insisting that she take it. Obediently she sipped a few spoonfuls and then lying back against the pillows she asked if she could have her sedative. I gave her the prescribed dose and then she asked me if I would leave the bottle of tablets beside her bed.

Her request startled me.

Noticing my reaction to her request, she whispered, 'Don't you trust me? It's just that I like to know they're there — for tomorrow night.'

'Sure,' I smiled. 'Like insurance, eh!' Placing the bottle on her bedside table I went to my own room and flung myself on the bed fully dressed.

I had meant to rest there just for a short time but I awoke with a jolt six hours later. My light was on? Of course! I had left it on! I was fully dressed? Of course! That was the way I had been when I lay down! Then — why had I woken up feeling so uneasy, so full of foreboding?

Those tablets! That bottle of tablets . . . I hurried into Molly's room and turned on the centre light. She lay curled up, like a child, her hands clasped against her cheek. So still, so . . .? Had she taken an overdose of tablets?

I picked up the bottle, almost knowing that I was too late and through my mind flashed the ugly thought that I could be placed in Ralph Moyston's position. I felt some sympathy for Ralph, then a flood of feeling for Molly took over, and my hand that was holding the bottle trembled. I saw that she was sleeping quietly and comfortably, and I counted the tablets.

When I realized that the full quota of tablets was still in the bottle I returned to my room, taking one tablet with me. After swallowing it I lay on my bed, and waited impatiently for the sedative to take effect. Just before sleep took over, I made up my mind not to go to work the following day. I would stay at home and take care of Molly.

CHAPTER THIRTEEN

WHEN JOHN stayed home from work I suspected that something was being withheld from me. Spending that Sunday lying in bed all day, sapped the little strength I had gained. I could not stand up, I tried to several times but ended up crumpled like a rag doll on the worn carpet by the bed. Each time John came in and lifted me back on to my bed.

The third time it happened he became quite angry. 'Molly,' he admonished, and his voice came from behind tightly stretched lips, 'if you attempt to get out of bed again I'm calling the doctor and *telling him to cart you off to hospital*!'

I caught at his hand and promised that I would not get out of bed again. My promise was sincere for I was frightened that he would keep his word.

I had noticed a new weariness in him. It seemed to me that John rather hoped that I would disobey and then he would be free of me, at least for a while. I am terribly sorry for John. He has been so contented, so satisfied, in a way for the past year. I suspected that it was because òf his friendship with Miss Prentice.

Had she gone away? Was she still at the library and had she and John lost interest in each other? I was certain that on John's side that was not so. I felt that his depression was connected with a break between them, whatever it was. I was distressed that John's happiness had gone from him, and suddenly, I felt that I had to know why and there was a way of finding out! If I could have the house to myself I would telephone the library.

I waited until three o'clock, then, 'John!' I called, in a

lively, cheerful voice and he came at once. He stood in the doorway, saying, 'Yes, dear?'

I smiled, 'John, it is the queerest thing — but — John, I would like a dish of chocolate ice-cream. I have quite a craving for it.'

'My goodness!' John was so surprised, and so was I for I had not heard him use that expression for years, then he said that he would go and buy some at once and when he had left the house I crept from my bed.

I wobbled along the hallway and into the living room. I had not used the telephone for months. I had not even glanced at the number-pad. Only a few numbers had been added to it and all in John's firm, square handwriting.

The library number was not amongst them and I was just about to lay the pad down when I noticed that the last number on the list was the Railway Hotel, and beside the name of the hotel and its telephone number, John had written, 'Ralph'!

Steadying my mind, I looked at the pad again and I saw that John had not written firmly, but had scribbled the name, Gorman, several times.

Without clear thought and before I realized what I was doing, I dialled the Railway Hotel number and clearing my throat, nervously, I spoke to the answering switch girl, asking, 'May I speak with Mr Moyston, please!'

'We have no one registered under that name —' Before the girl had time to cut me off, I asked, 'Then, Ralph Gorman, please . . .'

'He's not taking any more calls,' the girl said coldly. 'Are you from the Press?' The girl cut me off.

The Press . . .? What had happened? Was there something about Ralph in the newspaper? I do not bother to read the papers any more, and John had never got around to replacing the television and radio. Had there been something about Ruth?

I had not replaced the telephone receiver and I watched

the black cord slide, like a snake, across my worn, faded nightdress.

The walls of the living room began to close in on me, and as they hit me on all sides, I called out, 'Oh, God — poor Ralph! Poor Ralph!'

CHAPTER FOURTEEN

MOLLY'S REQUEST for ice-cream was unexpected and it sent me scurrying to buy it. I also bought pipe tobacco and two evening newspapers and tucking them under my arm, I started the trek homewards.

Before reaching the corner of our street, I stumbled and the papers fell to the sidewalk. Picking them up I saw the headlines, and I walked back in the direction from which I had just come. On reaching a bus seat, I sat down and saw a photo of Ralph Moyston splashed on the front page. I thought it was a poor likeness of Ralph.

Beneath his photo was a luridly written account of the police calling Ralph in for questioning about the disappearance of his wife, 'who' so the article read, 'had disappeared from her home under mysterious circumstances.'

I read the trashy article through, disgusted by the over-exaggerated account of Ruth having left her home, and as I went on my way, I was even more convinced that Grey was mistaken in his suspicions about Ralph.

I decided not to take the papers home with me. Molly would be extremely upset if she read the article. She had always liked Ralph so much, and so had I. I still liked him, and I still believed in him. I sympathized with him and I hoped that the entire affair would just fizzle out and leave Ralph to make a life for himself with the woman he was living with. I thought him a fool to have made the mistake of applying for a marriage licence, but maybe the woman was pregnant. The thought occurred to me that — living or dead — Ruth Moyston would always be a drag on Ralph.

My amoral attitude startled me, and, dropping the newspapers into the gutter, I hurried on home, only to discover Molly lying on the living room floor.

God! I had believed for several moments that she had died! Then, realizing that she had fainted and was out cold, I called the doctor. The fact that the telephone receiver was lying on the floor beside Molly had not registered with me at the time, but later, much later, I wondered who Molly had been trying to call.

The doctor! Perhaps she had been trying to call the doctor? I never found out. The doctor was seriously concerned and called for an ambulance to take Molly to the hospital. Whilst awaiting the ambulance, with a heavy heart I packed Molly's two frayed nightgowns into an old case, along with a few other necessities, and I spent that night waiting at the hospital.

Grey arrived about midnight and stayed with me for a few hours. He was extremely sympathetic. We spoke very little and he did not mention Ralph and neither did I. I asked about Jodie, and Grey said that she was completely broken up and that Rob was also deeply upset.

For a week I spent my days, and nights, between home, work and the hospital. I was in a peculiar state of deep depression and every moment I expected to hear that Molly had passed away. The doctor, from the beginning, had been gravely concerned about the condition of her heart. I did not like the doctor's attitude towards me. It was accusatory, rude, for he had decided that Molly was a neglected, browbeaten wife and that I was an unkind, callous husband.

On the sixth day, the head nurse approached me as I sat in the gloomy waiting room, saying sombrely, 'You can see Mrs Blake now — if you wish.'

'If I wish?' I stammered. 'See her! Is she —?' I was sure that Molly must have passed away and to my shame I felt no emotion at all, then the nurse spoke even more sombrely, saying, 'There has been a great improvement. It was unexpected. We are delighted, Mr Blake.'

I do not think that I was delighted but I was thankful.

I no longer have any love for my wife, but I do have a deep and abiding pity for her and there is nothing I would not do to help her live on for years, in, at least, a happier frame of mind than the one she has lived in for so long.

I have given up my job. I have some money put by, and I have confidence that somehow the property will be sold and there will be more than enough money to buy a new place, live on, reasonably, until I find a new job. When Molly is brought home from the hospital I will employ a woman to come in and care for her. Maybe I will even find work that will really interest me. I am not yet senile; I am forty-seven and my health is excellent.

My heart? My heart is heavy and devoid of any expectation of personal happiness.

Grey and I both agreed, that, in a way, it was a good thing having Molly in the hospital, but when she was able to sit up and take an interest in the life about her, then, Grey suggested, that I have her brought home as soon as permission could be obtained.

'Get a nurse in your home, John,' he said firmly. 'We don't want Mrs Blake hearing things. At home, you can keep any upsetting news that might arise from her until she is strong enough to deal with it.'

I agreed, not believing that any further upsetting news would arise. Grey asked me, curiously, why it was that both Molly and I thought so highly of Ralph Moyston. I told him that Ralph had always been a pleasant and a most self-effacing man and . . .

He shrugged and said that in his opinion we were certainly not good judges of character. We left it at that.

Molly is home, and a nurse comes in every day from nine in the morning till four in the afternoon. She is a pleasant woman, quite impersonal, and seems satisfied with the conditions in our home, but to me the place has a cold, sad smell.

I have warned the nurse that no newspapers are to be given to Molly. All news about Ruth and Ralph has fizzled out just as I had expected.

Whilst Molly was in hospital the Moyston home and yard was gone over by detectives. They came into my house too and questioned me several times. I had no information to give them and at last we are being left in peace.

I went into the city one day, going to the Railway Hotel, but although Ralph was still registered there he had not been in. Following that visit I had attempted to reach him by telephone on several occasions but always failed to catch him. On those occasions I had left my name requesting that he should call me back but he had not bothered to call. I did not blame him, feeling that if I had been in his shoes I would not want to be troubled by people, who, in most cases, would be merely curious and even interfering.

I went to call on Jodie and for the first time in years, she spoke bitterly about her mother. She thinks always and only about her father, telling me that she had seen him on several occasions and saying, quite cheerfully, 'Uncle John, Daddy is as cool as a cucumber! I met his girlfriend and she's real nice! Daddy deserves some happiness after the hell my mother put him through. Well, he was loving to me, even laughing and he told me not to worry even one jot about the stupid way the police are treating him. You know, like making him report to them and things like that.'

Jodie, like myself, had utter confidence in Ralph. However, it was not quite like that with her husband, Bill, or with young Rob. They seem fascinated by the situation and seem rather proud of the newspaper article about Ralph. Grey tells me that such attitudes are not unusual. Many people, he says, no matter what the circumstances, delight in being connected with the news media, as though it gives them a mantle tinged with fame.

'Haven't you ever noticed, John,' he grinned, 'how people, especially women, doll themselves up when they appear as a witness in the Courts? They do, and it's a sick thing to see.'

Life has taken on a steady, dull routine. My only relaxation is taking long morning walks before Molly awakes.

The nurse comes, the nurse goes.

I give Molly her supper. I have my own, I wash the dishes and sit about the house until it is time to go to bed.

Whenever he is able to, Grey comes over and sometimes we play chess. I know that he is convinced of Ralph's guilt, but apart from a personal interest he is not involved in the case. I am thankful that he no longer brings the subject up with me, for I am sick and tired of the drawn-out, distasteful business. Ralph is no longer mentioned in the newspapers. A sensational double murder has occurred and the police, the press, and public, are full of it.

Molly is becoming stronger every day. I suppose that it is only in my imagination but I feel that she is trying to build herself up for something. There is a stubborn tenaciousness in the way she slowly chews at her food, as though determined to draw strength from it. We have become a strangely impersonal couple with no interests in common.

I am borrowing books from Grey, losing myself again in the world of reading and the monotony of my life is almost pleasing as I move through each day, suspended, without ambitions and without any thoughts other than those of living the day through and sleeping the night away.

Sometimes, Grey and I sit on canvas chairs in the back garden, by the kitchen door. The garden is beginning to take on a sadly neglected appearance with flowers withering away on their stalks, and weeds crowding up between the shrubs. The grass is badly in need of attention.

No one but the nurse, the tradesmen, and Grey, sometimes, ever call to the house. But this morning one of the women from the apartment house came over to the dividing fence and called to me, asking if she could come in and pick a few flowers from the garden.

'Go ahead,' I told her. 'Pick as many and as often as you wish to.'

Molly is now able to walk about the house. She never gets herself fully dressed but wears a soft blue robe that I bought for her. Occasionally I have heard her moving about in the kitchen when Grey and I were in the garden, and I never bothered to check, to see what she was after, because she is really well enough now to do more than she is doing.

I leave her to herself, hoping that she will regain more confidence and eventually be less dependent and less of a drag on me.

CHAPTER FIFTEEN

I AM PLEASED to be alive. God is merciful! I repeat again and again, God is merciful, because He is prolonging my life when the doctors had despaired of it. If I had died, I would not be alive to clear Ralph.

I have given up thinking of the hereafter. I have made up my mind not to dwell on thoughts like that, but to go on building up my strength, and then, to confess to Mr Grey that Ralph is innocent; entirely, utterly and completely innocent.

Young Nurse Phillips thinks of me as the ideal patient. With a determination that amazes me, I eat when she tells me to eat, struggling through plates of food that I do not want. I drink milk and swallow my pills and I suffer my vitamin injections with never a flinch. I allow my hair to be brushed and my nails to be cut. I suffer the agony of having a talcum powder sprinkled on my body, powder with a perfume that nauseates me, reminding me of the flowers I was forced to cultivate.

'Don't you like this perfume?' Nurse Phillips queried solicitously, 'Would you prefer violet? I — myself — adore this carnation.'

'Me too,' I lied, 'I adore it. I adore this carnation perfume.'

When she, Nurse Phillips, had been with me for several weeks I began to encourage her to talk about herself. She talked about herself and about nothing else from that time on. It surprised me that a young woman with such a simple past, present, and, I imagine, future, could find such interest in her own doings and likes and dislikes. There is no end to them. She is utterly fascinated with herself.

I began to listen, not to what she was saying but to the soothing tone of her voice. I think she enjoys being my nurse. In the weeks she has been with me I have made only one request, and of course, when I eventually made it, she felt, as I had planned, that she could not refuse me, saying, 'Oh, yeah, I guess I can manage that for you, Mrs Blake. I don't see why not. My father, you know, I told you how my Dad can never bear to throw anything away, well, I'm sure we have all the newspapers from way back piled up in his workshop. You know, I told you about Dad's workshop.'

The following day she brought me the newspapers that I had asked for.

'Please put them in the bottom drawer of my dresser, Nurse,' I requested. 'I shall read them later on, I don't want Mr Blake to know that you've brought them. You'll remember that, won't you?'

'Oh, sure,' she replied, and went on to tell me of the young man she had met at a friend's house and how he, Peter, had called her and how she was going to the theatre with him. 'We are going to a restaurant first, then on to the show.'

As she babbled on I had a feeling that the story she was telling me was one that I had heard before. As her voice droned on I closed my eyes. I knew she was anxious to leave so that she could put her hair in rollers, beautify herself for her big date, so when I suggested that she leave an hour earlier she was off and away almost before I had finished speaking to her.

Now, there was only John to manage. I knew that it was useless to ask John to leave the house because he no longer had any confidence in my word since discovering me lying unconscious on the floor. It is strange that he has never asked me why I had used the telephone that day. Maybe I *had* put the receiver back. I must have done so. My memory is hazy about that time.

112

Although I was quite desperately wanting to read those newspapers I knew there was nothing to do but wait until night. When at long last John was in bed and asleep I got up, closed my door and I took those newspapers out of the drawer: Nurse Phillips, for all her shortcomings, is efficient. She had brought the editions I wanted so much.

There was only one edition that was important. Ralph's photograph was splashed on its front page . . .

I have looked at that photographed face many many times. I have read that article about Ralph many many times.

My admiration of Ralph grows and flourishes and I long to see him, to speak with him, tell him that I am going to give myself up and that he will be cleared of all suspicion, free to give up his protection of me. My insurmountable problem is that I must see him, *talk with him*, before I make my confession, because I have no intention of telling the entire story.

My part in it, yes. Everything — but why should I tell of Ralph and of his part in it? He is innocent. I am guilty. Why then, should his strange actions, done only to prevent more violence, why should they ever be known? I again firmly made up my mind that his past would never be known and so I have to see, to talk with Ralph. I must find out if he is still living at that hotel.

Nothing must go wrong with these, my final plans. I have put all thoughts of John out of my mind. I know that he will not be as cruelly hurt as he would have been had the shocking information come to him a few years earlier. I not only suspect that I have become a tiresome burden to him — I know that I have . . .

I have made my plans and, as once before, I feel a release from my burdens and I enjoy a clarity of mind and a confidence of peace to come.

In being able to make my plans my main problem had been to get John away from his wearisome surveillance of my life. All I was wanting to do was to have the privacy of being allowed to make several telephone calls. Days went by and then — as often happens in life — a very simple incident gave me the chance I had been awaiting.

Nurse Phillips had already left the house and John sat reading in the living room. From my bedroom window I watched as a woman came into our garden. I had noticed her before and I knew that she was coming to pick some flowers.

These days, I never look at the garden. I always look beyond it, or up to the sky, but I watched that woman and I saw her trip and fall over the hose that lay carelessly unrolled. I heard her call out in pain as she attempted to rise. She has sprained her ankle, I thought, and I recalled the day I had sprained *my* ankle.

'John,' I called urgently, 'John, that woman — the one who likes flowers — she is in some kind of trouble . . .'

At once, John went outside to the garden and as he assisted and helped the woman hop and hobble down our overgrown path and back to the apartment building, I realized that my chance had come. Calling the Railway Hotel, I was told that, yes, Ralph Gorman was still registered there, and that, yes, it was customary for him to leave for his work around about nine every morning. The switch girl was casual and disinterested. I hung up, and then I called a cab company.

I already knew the cab company's telephone number. I had memorized it for this occasion. The girl on the switchboard said that the cab I was ordering would be on time in the morning. 'Yes,' she said, 'exactly at the corner. Yes, *exactly* at eight o'clock tomorrow morning. Are you catching a train — a plane?' she had queried.

I told the girl that I would inform the cab driver of my destination in the morning. I asked the switch girl was it really necessary for her to know? She replied saying that the drivers like to know beforehand where they were going and how long they would be needed.

Patiently, I reiterated that I wanted the cab at the corner of the street and I told her that I would need the cab for at least two hours. The switch girl finally said it would be as I wished.

Exhausted and nervous, I went back to my room. I had confidence that my plan would work. Since giving up his job, John has developed the habit of taking early morning walks, I have only recently become aware of that and I knew that he would be away from the house when the cab picked me up.

I must be strong. *Yes, I must be strong!* Now that time is growing short, I must be clear-minded, concise, and courageous.

I am finding it difficult to stop trembling and shaking and it is difficult to keep my mind clear, but I know that this is only natural for I do have a dreadful ordeal ahead of me. A great ordeal because after I have spoken with Ralph, I will come home, I shall sit in the living room, I shall tell John that it is very important that I see Mr Grey.

Mr Grey will arrive and he will look at me with that nice expression on his face, as if he did not find me a strange, unpleasant woman. Then — at once — I shall confess that *I* caused Ruth's death. That Ralph knows nothing about the matter. I will explain to Mr Grey, and he, Mr Grey, will believe me.

Yes, it will be a dreadful ordeal, but after — yes after — I will be free . . .

When John returned to the house he told me that the woman had merely twisted her ankle. He then asked me if I would like to have a glass of milk in bed or if I would be getting up again.

'I would like it in bed, please, John,' I said, but when he

brought the milk to me — together with a large piece of cake — I was unable to either eat or to drink. I thought that John would begin fussing, and that we would have to go through one of the artificial conversations we often indulged in since that ghastly evening by the rock-garden. I have always been embarrassed to meet his gaze since then because I know — that for that time, at least — I was insane and I know that John knows that too.

I wanted to get out of bed and wrap the uneaten food in a page from one of those newspapers that I keep hidden in the drawer, but my legs would not hold me up, so I stayed in bed with the tray on my lap. I was not too worried by the weakness and I remembered that this was my last day as a *person*. Tomorrow, I would be... yes, I would be an infamous woman — a woman who had killed and then had buried her victim's body and, and...

Yes, it was only natural that I could not eat, that I felt so weak and ill.

John merely smiled sympathetically as he took the tray away, saying, 'Not feeling hungry? Not feeling too good?' I smiled up at him, and it was queer, because when I went to the bathroom, I glanced into the mirror and the smile was still branded on my face...

Mr Grey had come over to chat with John. The two men were sitting on canvas chairs in the garden just by the back door.

Getting out of bed I put on my blue robe and I went to the kitchen doorway. I stood there looking at them and they looked very nice — both of them — they were two nice men, good men. I wanted to sit with them because for the first time in years, I was frightened to be alone. I needed, I wanted the warmth of the feeling of being with people, but I also felt terribly shy, and when Mr Grey looked up suddenly, and saw me standing there, I drew back quickly, but he stood up and held out his hand to me as though I

116

were a child, and, like a child, I made a little run towards him. He gave me his chair and drew up another chair for himself.

John looked rather surprised, but he smiled at me and I sat back with a feeling that, for the next hour at least, I was going to be like any other woman. Just an ordinary, middle-aged woman sitting with her husband and his friend.

A gentle peace surrounded me as I listened to John telling Mr Grey that he had recently had the feeling that he could write a novel. 'I'd like to have a shot at it,' he said, 'I would jolly well like to take a shot at it!'

'I'm not surprised, John,' Mr Grey smiled, 'I think you should have a go at it.'

John seemed enthusiastic and I listened, dreamily, as they talked on. An hour went by, one of the loveliest hours of my life. I lost track of the men's conversation, then, suddenly, John laughed and I began listening again as they talked on. John's voice comforted me. I have always liked his voice; I would not be hearing it after tomorrow . . .

He was telling Mr Grey about the woman who had come in to pick flowers. 'She was rather a tartar,' he laughed, 'She warned me that if her ankle were badly injured I would be up for damages.'

Mr Grey laughed too. 'People!' he said. 'There's no telling how they will act — or react. John, don't you think it rather a shame that this garden is going to such rack and ruin? All those fine plants, and after all Mrs Blake's years of dedicated work.'

He lowered his voice just a little. Mr Grey was still certain that unless he spoke clearly, loudly and directly to me, I would be unable to hear him.

'I haven't the slightest interest in this garden,' John replied, flatly. John seemed to have forgotten that I was sitting with them and his voice expressed resentment as he continued on, saying rather bitterly, 'I worked for years on this plot of land,' he gestured widely, 'For years, I spent every cent I could afford, and I worked on it, and —'

'*You* worked?' Mr Grey was astounded. 'You're joking! It is Mrs Blake who —'

'No,' interrupted John, 'Molly only took the garden over, after . . .' he stopped speaking as though he did not care when I had taken over.

They were both silent. The subject of the garden seemed to have lost interest for them. I was relieved — very relieved. Then, John said thoughtfully, 'I've just remembered! The last plants that I personally bought and planted in the garden were those three camellia bushes . . .'

His forefinger stabbed in the direction of the rock-garden. 'I was so proud of them . . .' he gave a long, queer sigh. 'Especially, I was proud of the perfect — perfectly white blooms — of the bush in the centre. The two pinks are lovely, but that white was my pride and my joy . . .'

The three of us sat and stared at John's camellia bushes. They were in full bloom. Flowers covering them in rich profusion. I had not even noticed that they were in bloom.

Suddenly, I shivered, remembering the many times I had nipped the buds from the bushes. I stopped shivering because I did not mind any more and seeing how really beautiful they were I felt a small pang of regret, knowing that soon the camellia bushes would be uprooted again.

'But, John,' said Mr Grey, 'Are you colour-blind? Take a look, man! The flowers on the bush in the centre are pink! The *white* one is on the right of it.'

'So it is!' murmured John. 'So it is! But . . .?' His voice trailed into silence, then, 'But — this is crazy . . .' he whispered, 'Grey, someone must have moved, uprooted, *replanted* them . . .'

John sprang to his feet and he became very excited. Mr Grey stood up too and he also became very excited. He caught at John's arm, they stared at one another, their mouths agape, 'John, are you sure? Are you . . . certain?' asked Mr Grey and his voice was as cold as my hands.

My hands were growing colder and colder with every passing second . . .

'By Christ, I am certain!' said John, and without another word Mr Grey went into the house, and I heard the tiny ting of a bell as he lifted the telephone receiver before dialling a number.

The cold was spreading throughout my body, and as though from a great distance, I heard the mumble of Mr Grey's voice, and I heard John using words I had never heard him use before — filthy words — as he spoke about Ralph Moyston. Then — as Mr Grey came running from the house — John crossed the garden and like a madman he began to tear and tug at the proud camellia bushes which resisted his efforts with all the strength they had garnered over the years from that which lay buried beneath them.

Mr Grey ran for shovels, and like two demented children digging at the beach, John and Mr Grey dug the camellia bushes up and flung them aside.

I could not move from the old canvas chair . . . No one would ever believe me now, believe that tomorrow, I had been going to confess . . . Ralph would be heavily implicated, Ralph could be blamed entirely. Who would believe the prattling of a frozen woman?

I had failed! It was too late now . . . Too late . . . Those little mewing sounds began again, like hiccoughs, like a lost kitten's cries . . .

No one noticed me. Perhaps those men erupting from the police cars that had screamed up sharply in the front of our house thought of me as a kitten? Or a cat, a big cat . . .?

But I was not a cat! I was Molly, Molly Blake, a woman.

Somehow, I got to my feet and I limped slowly, but very steadily towards the rock-garden and I stood amidst the

119

group of excited men and I watched, as John and Mr Grey now watched, whilst two of the policemen began to dig deeper — deeper.

Except for the sound of the digging, the garden was silent with ugly curiosity, with wild interest, for they were not yet quite sure — not quite — and a strange odour, instead of nauseating them, as it nauseated me, seemed to add fuel to their fires of energy.

Yes, they were like ghouls, all of them. I hated them, all of them. All of them. 'Stop . . .!' I said. 'Stop digging — listen to me . . .'

John, who was still holding a shovel, turned and looked at me. 'Molly,' he cried in great distress, 'Molly — darling, go inside the house! You must not see.'

Darling! John, calling me darling . . .!

'John,' I whispered, 'You must listen to me. Please, dear John, *please* listen to me . . .'

Two of the uniformed men moved towards me. One of them took my arm, intending I suppose, to lead me into the house, but Mr Grey said, sharply, 'Let Mrs Blake say what she feels she must.' He came to my side and wiping his soiled hand against his trousers he put an arm about me, saying, 'Molly, I believe I know what you are about to say.'

He had used my name for the first time and I leant thankfully against his strength and I looked up into his eyes. They were still kind, kinder than usual.

'Molly,' he questioned, 'You have known all along, haven't you? You have known that Ralph Moyston killed his wife and that he . . .'

He gestured to the chaos at our feet as he continued, saying, ' . . .Ruth Moyston's body is buried there . . .' he pointed downwards. 'You have known all along — haven't you?'

'Yes,' I said. '*Yes*,' I repeated. 'I have known — all along.'

Amid the sudden hum and the buzz of voices about me, I heard another voice, unearthly and deep with sorrow.

Only *I* heard that voice, I think that it was the voice of, I think that it was the voice of my God, for it told me that from now on there was no hope of redemption for me.

Too late, too late . . .

I had laid the blame of Ruth's murder on Ralph. I had not meant to — just as I had not meant to kill Ruth.

The figure of John appeared to change into a smaller, weaker figure, into that of Ralph Moyston, as he had stood on the same spot John now stood on, holding the same shovel. Suddenly, I sprang at John and I struggled with him, attempting to drag the shovel away from him.

After an instant, he let me hold the shovel, saying, 'I'll take her inside. She is quite unstrung! *Quite unstrung.*'

'Yes,' I cried, 'Yes, take me into the house, take me into the house, John, I am — as you say — unstrung . . .'

I noticed that people were leaning from the windows of the apartments next door, and that strangers were crowding into the back yard of John's home. John, everyone, felt pity, felt sympathy towards me.

But — how about Ralph? Yes, how about Ralph?

'John,' I said — loudly, clearly — 'Before you take me inside, I must tell you that *I* dug this hole, four years ago. That *I* dug it myself. That *I* killed Ruth. That *I* dragged her across the gardens. That *I* buried her and her clothes and the photograph of Jodie and Rob. And her handbag. *I* took the money from Ruth's handbag, and weeks later *I* gave it to Ralph, telling him that I had found it on the path the day that Ruth disappeared. John, *I* did *everything* all by myself and *I* will tell you now — tell you all — before you dig any further and come upon Ruth. I will tell you exactly what you will find. You will find Ralph's old brown suitcase that *I* took from the top of the wardrobe. In it, you will find Ruth's jewel case, her . . . You will find her toothbrush, her smashed broken glass. Her medicine bottle . . . her medicine bottle . . . her medicine bottle. Her . . .'

Would no one stop me? Had they not heard enough? No.

They wanted more! Like an audience at a good performance, they wanted more. On and on, on and on and I, like a stuck recording, went on and on. 'Her medicine bottle . . . her med'. . .'

Still no one spoke or moved, but a bird flew over the garden, a great blackbird. I fell silent. My eyes followed the bird's flight. Then I looked at John, I loved John — so much. I loved him.

'John,' I whispered, and I held out my hands to him, 'John — help me . . .'

John turned his back on me.

I think it was Mr Grey who carried me into the house. Yes, it was Mr Grey. I sat watching him dial a number on the telephone.

For an instant, one part of my mind became vividly alive. I had confessed. Ralph has been cleared.

That, at least, I had done . . .

CHAPTER SIXTEEN

I AM NEVER absolutely certain that truth is stranger than fiction, but as a police officer, and as an avid reader, I am certain that one work of fiction, Dostoyevsky's immortal novel Crime and Punishment, *continues to have enormous influence on those studying the psychology of the criminal mind. His humanitarian ideology has always tempered my thought processes towards understanding the characters and the motives of those who have been caught up into the sordid realms of brutality and crime. However, not even the genius of Dostoyevsky has helped me to puzzle out the Moyston affair to my complete and personal satisfaction.*

Mrs Blake died on the day of the inquest into the death of Ruth Moyston. I was glad when Molly died, glad that she was finally at peace. Nevertheless, I am overcome by a sense of uneasiness whenever I think of her.

Her frenzied but coherent documentary of the crime she had committed left me in no doubt that she had been deeply involved in the murder of the Moyston woman, yet, I am consistently being niggled by the thought that somewhere along the line the whole truth has not been told. There are times when I am oppressed by certain memories of Molly, memories which are clear and sharp and always she appears to me as a decent, likeable woman incapable of violence.

I become irritated, feel that I have lost my touch, failed in my chosen field of work and I thrust the memories away but they recur, pricking my conscience. I feel that I should have paid more attention to her as she went her way, sloggingly, hefting heavy loads, creating a garden of fantastic beauty, not, as it had appeared to me, for her own pleasure, but in fact as a terrified woman covering up evidence of a heinous crime.

She had never had any actual reasons to fear me for I had little professional interest in the fate of Ruth Moyston, but did she, Molly, always believe that I had been on her trail? Out to catch and accuse her of murder?

In a strange, quite painful way, I hope she did not feel like that. But, if so, I feel a real right bastard, knowing that if I had been more on the ball I could, in all probability have gained her confidence, shortened her agonized time of waiting for the inevitable axe to fall: Nothing else, of course, but at least that would have been much better for her.

It would suit me down to the ground if I could simply file my memories away, out of sight and out of mind, but even after two years the Moyston case keeps cropping up, filling my mind with perplexities. I have never understood why John Blake took so many years before noticing that those three camellia shrubs had been interfered with. And why had Molly, herself, not realized the fact and done something about it? Had she left them as they were, waiting, even hoping, to have the bright harvest of flowers shout her guilt and set her free from the life of incredible strain and terror she must have been living under?

There is no chance of solving my speculations, no use in attempting to delve into the actions and the mind of a person who is dead and buried. During all the years I had known Molly, I am able to recall only one time when I know that she had a moment of pure happiness before she was struck down. It was during that gruesome episode in the Blakes' garden, when the men were digging down, deep, into the rock-garden. Molly had risen from her chair and walked to stand by John, who, on suddenly becoming aware of her, cried out, protectively, 'Molly — darling! Go inside the house! You must not see . . .'

As he spoke, her expression flowered into a fleeting show of passionate, tender love, together with one of gratitude. For a reason I could not understand, I was deeply moved. Was it because John had spoken so lovingly and shown his concern for her?

Perhaps I am being fanciful! It lasted but a moment, to be completely overshadowed by the grisly, appalling events which followed and left her broken and devastated.

In the ensuing chaos it was I, not John Blake, who carried Molly's thistle-light body from the garden into the house; placing her on a chair whilst I telephoned to Headquarters. She had sat watching me, silent, as still as death itself, then all at once she astonished me by saying, clearly, succinctly, and as though with a great content, 'That — at least — I have done!'

Try as I may, I am unable to fathom out her meaning. She made no further utterance and I could see that she was fast becoming lost to the reality of the world about her, and I did not trouble her for explanations, knowing that she was in a state of shock. I was shocked myself, more shocked and flabbergasted than ever before in my long career.

I stood by, watching as she was escorted from her home by two uniformed policemen, and I watched as she was driven away in a car with its siren blaring. I resented the crowd of curious, murmuring strangers looking on.

The shattering blow John Blake received that afternoon when his wife, a seemingly demented woman, caught at his arm for support, then spewed out her detailed story of horror left him a broken, stunned man. However, now, two years later, he has recovered. Quite recovered I must admit, and he has married again. Married a delightful woman, a librarian, who helps him run the book shop that he purchased from part of the proceeds he received from the sale of his property.

There could be a jinx on that land adjoining the apartment house I live in. Blake and Moyston made a packet when their properties were purchased, but so far all the real estate developer has done is to have bulldozed the two houses down, removed the rubble and then let Nature take its course. From my windows I look down and see a few bright-flowering shrubs amidst the weeds and tangles of vines that have flourished and taken over the beautiful garden that Molly Blake created.

I visit John and Lorraine occasionally. Molly's name is never *mentioned, which is understandable, but there are times when I am with the Blakes that I have an eerie feeling that Molly is also present. Again, I admit to being fanciful but the feeling persists.*

Ralph Moyston has also remarried. Yes, to the 'nice lady' whom Maisie, my barmaid pal, told me about that day in the disreputable pub.

I have been forced to eat crow where Ralph Moyston is concerned. On one occasion, whilst speaking with John Blake, John expressed admiration in that Moyston in no way felt any malice towards me. He also stressed the point that Moyston's behaviour in having lived under a false name to escape from memories of the harrowing life he had endured with his virago of a wife, was not a crime and that under similar circumstances, many a man would have acted as Moyston had. In all honesty, I had to agree.

I still find Moyston an unpleasant character, although I know that he is considered to be a gentle, peace-loving man. Certainly, Jodie loves him and her children adore their grandfather. I should find it a pleasing sight to watch young John at play and to see Jodie's baby girl snuggling, smiling and confident in Moyston's arms. They named the child Ruth, and she is said to be accident prone, or, as her young mother says, 'A child who bruises easily.'

Moyston has been completely exonerated. For myself, I wish that I could once and for all put out of my mind the expression that I believe I saw on his face — just for an instant — during the Coroner's Inquest.

John Blake, of course, along with Jodie, her husband and her brother, and with ghoulish members of the public who never miss out on a sensation — if they can get one for free — were present that day in the dim gloom of the Court House.

Although I had been no longer professionally involved in any capacity with the case, and was deeply involved with my own work, I took time out during the period before the Inquest to visit Molly in the prison hospital, and she seemed quite lost to reality. Indeed, I was amazed that she was considered sane and well enough to attend the Court. However, there she was, neatly dressed, sitting erect, between a policewoman and a prison hospital nurse.

During the proceedings, I noticed that Molly scarcely ever took her gaze away from John Blake's face, and I noticed that he, John, kept his own gaze averted, never looking in her direction. I suppose that he was acting as many people would act under such unhappy circumstances. He had been put through the wringer in no mean fashion, as the husband of a seemingly run-of-the-mill housewife who had turned out to be a monster of iniquity.

The murder of Ruth Moyston and, even more than that, the burying of her corpse and the beautification of the garden above and around the hidden grave, caught the public's imagination. The press and television camera crews had a bonanza and I believe that a paperback novel on the story is about to hit the market.

Only once, in that courtroom, did I see Molly's gaze move away from John's face. The report was being read about the cause of Ruth Moyston's death.

The body — *ran the report* — was in a bad state of decomposition . . . There was no evidence of any injury to the skull or elsewhere to indicate the cause of death . . . A medicine bottle containing potassium cyanide mixed with a stomach medicine had been found in the grave, and . . . .

Stunned at the mention of cyanide, my eyes went to Molly Blake and on her face I saw an expression — all encompassing — of . . . ? Of what? I have never been able to find words to describe that look, that expression. Was it shame? Guilt? Shock? Innocence? I shall never know.

Interrupting Court proceedings, she had struggled to her feet, crying out as though in an agony of remorse, 'Oh, dear God! What a fool, what a fool I was *. . .' Then, obviously in great pain and clutching at her chest, she had collapsed, falling to the floor.*

Pandemonium followed and as the Coroner called for order, the prison nurse who had been kneeling, attending to Molly, stood up, saying, starkly, 'Mrs Blake is dead!'

It was then — at that precise moment — I noticed that Ralph Moyston had risen to his feet and I firmly believe that I saw the expression of extreme trepidation on his face give way fleetingly to one of utter triumph and complacency. That momentary change of Moyston's expression created an explosion of suspicion in my mind.

I have been a policeman for more than twenty years and during those years I have been closely connected with many cases of homicide, but of all those I have dealt with, only one — Molly Blake's — haunts me.

I have an uneasy, an uncanny feeling that she is always trying to contact me, with a ghostly anguish, wanting to inform me of something I should know.